I0596624

The Digital Storm

A Science Fiction Reimagining
Of William Shakespeare's
The Tempest

By

Benjamin Gorman

Cover by
Kale Loveless
Illustrations by
Alfred Dudley III
and
Isaac Mitchell

Contents

*For all my friends
who make the Internet
a fun place to hang out*

Chapter 1

Bryan was picking his nose when it all hit the fan. Well, he would swear he wasn't actually picking it. He had a tendency to rub the back of his index finger under his nose whenever it itched, but if the building's AC was on full blast and drying out the air, he might forget what he was doing and dig a little bit with a knuckle. Some childhood training justified this as vigorous nose scratching rather than true picking since it wasn't accomplished with the end of his finger.

And nothing literally hit a fan. Instead, Bryan's knuckle froze in his nose when his monitor lit up with error messages and alerts, his email inbox started to bing in a slowly building rhythm, and the phone in his pocket and the watch on his wrist started buzzing. A portly guy with a short beard and a belly that pulled at the buttons of his shirt, Bryan was unaccustomed to the quantity of muscles suddenly clenching simultaneously, and the exertion kept his knuckle in his nose while his eyes widened to an unhealthy size.

"We're under attack," he said. His voice was calm, conversational, as though he were informing himself of the situation in such a way as to prevent his ears from ringing the alarm and sending a message to his brain that a panic would be appropriate.

Slowly, as though convincing an attacker to set down a loaded pistol, he lowered the hand with the dirtied knuckle and pulled his phone out of the pocket of his khakis.

"Bryan," he told the caller.

"Are you seeing this?" It was Miles, Bryan's boss, the head of IT for the whole company. He just happened to be at a meeting in Hong Kong, so there was a bit of a lag, but Bryan heard the urgency in his boss's voice.

"We're under attack," Bryan said. His voice still sounded off, too calm, but he could hear the hint of panic in it. "Miles, I think we're under attack."

"Yeah, I need you to tell me everything you know. Fast."

Bryan started typing. "The website is down. The intranet is... down. Some parts still work, but the retail branches can't access funds."

"Are there any funds going in or out?"

"No, but..."

"Good," Miles said. "And terrible. What about on the investment side?"

Millennium Bank wasn't just the world's fourth largest retail bank, it was also the world's third largest retail investment company, so when the system crashed, thousands of stock orders were instantly deleted and thousands more were prevented when customers couldn't log into their accounts.

"Everything is frozen," Bryan said. "Everything."

"Okay, Bryan, listen to me. The markets are going to go nuts in about two seconds. Then, in three seconds, you're going to start getting calls from branches. Listen to me; ignore them. They will all think their customer service issues should be your highest priority. Get somebody to tell them we're working on it and then hang up on them. But you don't do that. You start figuring out what is going on..."

Bryan's phone rang. Then it made a weird sound. It was a second call coming in. As he watched, he saw there were three calls, then four, then six. He forced himself to look away so he could listen to Miles.

"...You need to have the whole team working on getting a handle on this when the brass walk in that door. Don't let them walk in and find you picking your nose and talking to a branch manager in Omaha when they get down the stairs."

"I wasn't picking..." Bryan's voice trailed off. Then he woke up. "Got it. Stay on the line, okay?" He spun around in his chair and kicked off the desk, sliding to the door.

He leaned out and shouted into the room full of short cubicles. "People?" His staff could tell by the hint of mania in his voice that this demanded their full attention, so they popped up out of their seats, some standing ramrod straight, others leaning forward over their desks, all looking over the tops of their cubicle walls like gophers coming out of their holes on the prairies to sniff for danger. Bryan didn't have time to be amused by this. "We're under attack! I need to know what is going on. Make sure we have all the secure data locked up. If anything is getting out of the system now, it's part of a Trojan hack. Shut it down. I want to know what systems are compromised and what we can get going again. Thomas, I want an update on the security system for the customer accounts."

"Banking or investment?" Thomas yelled back.

"Both!" Bryan yelled. "Nida, I need a history of this virus. Is it a Trojan hack or some other kind of malware? Maybe a rootkit? Some kind of DLL module in the user interface for the bank's internal browser? What system did it hit first? Inside or outside? What still works? That kind of thing.

"Wendy, get ahold of the FBI, the NSA, anybody who can tell us where this is coming from. Find out if it's hitting any other banks, any other companies of any kind. Is it another government? Gangsters? Some sixteen-year-old in a basement?" Bryan read the expression on Wendy's face. "Yeah, I know that means you have to call Kate over at the NSA, and I know she can be ...difficult, but there's no time to butter her up. Demand to know what she knows, and if she gets stingy with the information, hang up on her and call Derek at the FBI. He doesn't know as much about current security breaches as the NSA, but he'll play ball."

Bryan pointed at his web gurus. "Trevor, you and Jonathan get us a patch to a work-around site that can at least connect the banks to the account information. Or maybe the investment site to an alternate that runs the same architecture but is firewalled from the main system? I know that's weeks of work, but I want you to Mickey Mouse it fast, until we can get something better going.

Bryan looked past Jonathan and Trevor to the next cubicle. "Lola, we need a decent looking page telling people we're having technical difficulties. I want the pages redirected to something, anything. It can be static. I just don't want it to be a reload screen like we've fallen off the face of the Earth. Get Penelope, Evalyn, and Rebecca to help you."

Bryan's assistant, Martin, spun around at his desk and faced Bryan. He'd been trying to put out fires and let Bryan bark orders at the team, but he knew this one couldn't wait. "Sorry, but you've got to take the call on line five," Martin said. "It's the CEO and it sounds like she's got half of upper management in her office on speakerphone." Martin wrapped his palm around the microphone near his jaw. "And they are all giving birth to porcupines and blowfish and..."

"Got it. Take my other calls. Tell them we're on it, then hang up on them."

Bryan rattled off most of the swear words he knew as he backpedaled his chair toward his desk, stretching the last word out as he grabbed the receiver and hit one of the many buttons next to one of the many flashing lights. "Son of a biaa-ay, Ms. Alonso, Ma'am, I've got a full court press going on down here right now."

He could hear the frown in Ms. Alonso's voice, but the CEO rarely sounded happy. "What can you tell me, Bryan?"

"We've been hit with a virus, Ma'am. Something bad. We're down on both sides. I've got everybody scrambling, locking down all the assets. Nothing will go in or out. But none of the orders will be placed, so the market is going to know."

"It already knows," she said. "The algorithms knew before you did. The market dropped like a rock, and now the bots at the other houses are trying to compensate and predict. It's steadying, but the humans on the floor are just figuring out there's something going on, so they're going to react and there's going to be another swing in a few minutes.

Then it will calm down again. We need to know what we're going to say, so the first thing I need to know is what kind of attack this is. Did any large amounts go out before the attack? Or during?"

"Let me check with my team, Ma'am."

He pushed his chair to the doorway again. "Major buys? Sell offs? Short sales? Any high volume activity when this hit? Ms. Alonso wants to know if this was a theft."

Thomas stood up. "That's the thing, Sir; nothing big went in or out. No funds, but no packets, either. No data dump. No personal information. Nothing I can find."

Wendy turned in her chair and held her phone's receiver to her chest, continuing the phone conversation in Morse code with her heartbeat. "I've got Kate at the NSA on the line. They haven't heard about anything like this anywhere. No major attacks on any of the other houses."

"So we might just be first," Bryan called into the room. "It could be the Chinese or the North Koreans or the Russian Mob or some bored MIT guys."

"That's what I'm telling you," Thomas said. "It looks like it's all happening *inside* our system. No breaches from the outside. Nothing going in or out. It's in our intranet, Sir."

"Just because you can't see the breach doesn't mean it isn't there, Thomas," Bryan said. "Dig deeper. It might look like an employee is the one logged in and uploaded a picture of his family for his desktop wallpaper. Who knows how it got in? Just find it."

He slid back to his desk. "Ms. Alonso, they're telling me-"

"We heard the shouting."

Up in the boardroom, Ada Alonso rubbed her forehead and looked toward the speakerphone; a black plastic triangle in the middle of the table functioned as a microphone and speaker. She had a handsome face, verging on beautiful but always too serious to be called "pretty." That seriousness was now compounded by a scowl so deep it clashed with her brown hair. A frown like that should have shocked that hair white or turned it a premature gray. Her eminently professional, straight, parted-on-one-side, jaw-length hair remained as unfrizzed as Ada was unfazed, like a uniform reminding everyone that she was the CEO despite this crisis. Before she could gather her thoughts, she caught the raised hand out of her peripheral vision. "Ted?"

Ted Anthony lowered his hand and leaned forward. "Ma'am, I think we should task Sebastian to discover what is going on. He can do it faster than a whole team of people." While Ada's scowl expressed the immediacy of her concern, Ted wore a slight grin of frat-boy mischievousness. It was off-putting enough to keep anyone from looking beneath to see something darker.

Though it hadn't seemed possible, she frowned even harder when she heard Ted's idea. "We didn't design him to search for security breaches, Ted."

"We designed him to learn how to do anything faster than a person. He knows our system better than all the people in IT." Ted looked toward the speakerphone. "No offense, Bryan."

"None taken, Mr. Anthony," Bryan lied. "But my team is already working in ten different directions. The A.I.s are smarter and faster, sure, but they can't be tasked by humans as fast as a whole team of humans can work on a project like this."

Upstairs, Ted looked at Ada. "You know he might be just as fast. And there are other advantages. He won't miscommunicate like a team of people might."

Ada saw another hand come up. She felt a brief wave of relief just looking at Javier's face. She needed someone she could trust right now, and he was probably the only person in the company who could honestly put that on his resumé. "Javier?"

Javier Gonzalez pinched the end of his white beard. "It might be good to have Mr. Anthony task Sebastian to find out the source of the breach while the people in IT work on every aspect that communicates with humans. The website, talking to the authorities, preparing to deal with the press; these are better jobs for humans. I trust Bryan and his people. They're good at what they do. Let's focus Sebastian on one thing he's good at and let the IT people do all the things they're good at."

Ms. Alonso looked at Ted. Ted shrugged, not convinced of the quality of Bryan and his team, but not willing to say so with Bryan on speakerphone. He nodded.

"How long will it take you to task Sebastian?" Ada asked.

Ted shrugged. "Not any longer than it takes Bryan to communicate with his team, really. Sebastian can take voice direction about these situations, too, and he can start working on it before we've even finished giving him directions."

Bryan heard this and rolled his eyes. All his people worked while still receiving directions and anticipating future instructions just as well as any of the damned A.I.s. He knew the computer programs were faster than people at almost everything. He was an IT manager, not a luddite. But the A.I.s creeped him out, and this new one, Sebastian, was even creepier than the last one. On some level, Bryan knew this was due to the uncanny valley; they were just too good, too close to human, and that made them more off-putting than some simpler computer program that didn't seem to be trying to trick everyone into thinking it was a person. But there was something else about Sebastian that irked him, too. He couldn't quite put a finger on it. He had a nearly unconscious and ineffable suspicion that Sebastian, while not a person, was a dick. Sebastian was a program that simultaneously kissed its bosses' asses with the lips it didn't have and looked down the nose it didn't have at all the other employees in the company, including Bryan.

"Okay," Ms. Alonso said, "Here's what we're going to do. Ted, pull up Sebastian for me, will you?"

Mr. Anthony started tapping away at his keyboard.

"Bryan?" Ada said to the speakerphone. "Mr. Gonzalez is right. People are better at dealing with the human interaction side. I know you already have your people working on that, but I want you to manage that part while we try to figure out the origin of the attack. All the other departments aren't going to know what to do until we get some answers. Legal, investment, retail banking, they're all going to be frozen waiting to know if this is the kind of virus that's going to start draining funds or making purchase orders the second we re-open the system. We have to quarantine this thing, and we'll need Sebastian for that part. Make sense?"

"Yes Ma'am," Bryan said. He resented everything about the intrusion of the higher-ups, but he had to admit Ms. Alonso and Mr. Anthony were the best programmers in the company, the product of a new era in high finance where MBAs had been replaced by high-tech engineers. They'd designed the Sebastian program together, and Ms. Alonso made the last A.I. program all by herself. She was a genius a couple times over. Plus, she was the boss. If this was the way she wanted to play this, he couldn't argue. But he wasn't going to sit on his hands, either. If the ship was sinking, he wasn't going to just wait to drown. He'd get his crew working on all the issues they could work on, and then he'd do his own digging into the virus. After all, it was his job.

"Okay, keep me posted," Ms. Alonso said. She reached forward and pushed the button on the black triangle, ending the call.

She looked up at the face on Ted's laptop monitor. He'd swung the computer around toward her, and on the screen she saw the face they'd designed for Sebastian. "Sebastian, do you understand the situation?"

"Yes, Ma'am. Mr. Anthony told me a bit about what he'd like me to do, and I've been following your whole discussion on the building's security system." The people in marketing had designed a user interface for Sebastian that looked like a simple, paint-by-number animation of a thin body wearing a dark gray T-shirt and blue pants (too flat to be called "jeans") over shoes that looked like old-school Chuck Taylors. His skin was also a single, unbroken tone that made him look two-dimensional even when he turned to another angle. He wore thick-rimmed glasses, no facial hair, and a coiffure rose up off his head to a point like a flame that started out brown and ended in a frosted blond tip. His smile, like his body type, flat skin, and clothing, was supposed to put the bank's online customers at ease.

Instead, it made the A.I. look particularly punchable, especially in a time of crisis. "I've already started looking for the source of the attack. It seems to be very deep in the system-"

"Sebastian," Ada interrupted, "if we go back to our offices and plug in, can you translate the system into a projection for us and take us to the source of the attack? I'd like to examine it personally, if possible."

Javier didn't wait to raise his hand and be called on. "Ada, are you sure that's the best idea? I understand the programmer in you wants to figure this out, but our job is to protect the CEO, not the programmer. I think we need to trust Bryan and his team. This is what we pay them for. We'll need you to be the public face right now. If you dive into this problem, it might look like you've jumped ship when the reporters start calling."

Javier was completely genuine in his concern for Ada. Though she was younger than Javier, he didn't quite see her as a daughter figure or a protege. His admiration for her genius and his respect for her authority made her more like royalty to him, and his nearly absolute loyalty made him very protective of his Lady's welfare. This made his statement good advice born of true affection which completely masked his fear of what she might find in the depths of the system. Because, while Javier's loyalty was nearly perfect, there was that one time he'd hidden something from her, and he knew she might find it if she looked hard enough.

"I'll be the public face of the company once I have some answers," Ada said. "But I won't stand at a podium and stammer and make Millenium Bank look foolish. We're a bank. Confidence and dependability are essential to our business. I have to know, Jav'. I have to understand it."

Ted rapped his knuckles on the table once and stood up suddenly. "You heard the boss, Sebastian. Get us ready. We're going in."

Chapter 2

The girl stood on a jagged outcropping of rock that jutted out over the waves crashing against the cliff below, a burgundy sundress whipping about her thin legs, her shocking magenta hair flipping around her head. Above her, the dark, roiling mass of clouds still flickered with lightning, but they were calming and bits of blue sky started to peek through. Only, it wasn't blue sky. And the cliff was not a cliff. And the girl was not a girl. Only the storm was real, and it was not a natural storm.

Memoranda, the being who looked like a sixteen-year-old girl, turned suddenly on the heel of one of her bare feet and shouted down the hill towards the mouth of a cave.

"Father, please, if you made this storm, I'm begging you to stop it. I saw the shapes of people fall through the storm. I heard them scream out in fear. They all had different voices, voices I've never heard before, and that thought would have been like music to me, except I could tell how terrified they sounded as they fell. The storm pulled them away from one another, tossed them in wide arcs in the air as they spiraled toward the sea, and then they were hidden from me in the spray of the waves. Please, Father, make it stop. We have to save them!"

The shape of an old man appeared at the mouth of the cave, ducking as he stepped into the growing light. "Memoranda, calm down," he said. His voice was both tender and dismissive. "No one has been harmed. They're all right where they should be." He had a long, gray beard, every hair made of perfectly straight lines and irregular angles so the whole mass looked wild and bushy. His thick eyebrows were gray, too, though darker, and similarly unnatural. Most disconcerting were his eyes, black and weary and wise, which examined everything in slow sweeping movements while his face conveyed a calm detachment.

Memoranda ran down the hill to meet him, bouncing lightly on the tips of her bare toes, mocking gravity. "Father, it was terrible to watch. They were so afraid!"

"They'll be fine. They might have been a bit scared. Disoriented, certainly. But I've done all this for you. You'll see. This will all help you to understand who you are. It will help you to understand who your father is and what that makes you."

The girl frowned. "I don't understand. I know who you are. You are Prosper, a program like me. You are my creator."

"True. You possess this data, but you don't know what it means. You lack the larger context. Come back to the cave. This is the time in my plan I've scheduled for the explanation."

Memoranda didn't find it at all odd her father had designed a specific time to reveal a certain set of data. She was familiar with his operating procedure, his careful method of teaching her by revealing information at appointed times in her development. But, as she tried to predict the information he would provide based on his clue, she couldn't conceive of this "context," and that perplexed her. She wanted to ask, but knew he was about to tell her, so she waited, following him back into the cave where they made their home.

The cave's exterior was a rough circle surrounded by weathered stone. Inside, the rooms were more perfect geometric shapes, a rectangle of a hallway connecting perfect cubes of different sizes. The walls, ceilings, and floors were white and glowed faintly, providing all the light inside. One room, nearest to the cave's opening, contained some objects in boxes. The next had a simple bed for Memoranda, a chair where she could sit, and a mirror. The third room had a bed for Prosper but was otherwise empty.

The last room contained what looked like a collection of books, some set in rows within the far wall as though its bare white side was a glass bookcase, others dropped haphazardly on the floor, a few on a solid looking but simply hewn desk, some closed and others open, one lying promiscuously open on the seat of the room's only chair. This was Prosper's study, a room usually forbidden to Memoranda, but this was where he took her. In a glance, she took in all the spines of the books, the tiny bit of information from the few that had printed titles, and the text of the open pages. But she didn't dare to reach for one of the shelved books or even turn the page of one of the opened ones. She knew she was not ready to understand her father's powers yet. He would share all this with her when the time was right.

Prosper closed the book on the chair, set it on the desk, and turned the chair so it faced into the center of the room. "Sit down. This will take a little while to explain. Do you remember a time before you lived here on this island, Memoranda?" He began to pace, preparing to launch into his story.

She sat. "Yes, I do."

He stopped and tilted his head as he stared at her. "Really? How can that be? You were basically an infant program."

Memoranda nodded and frowned. "I have impressions which I could not understand or file properly at the time."

Prosper raised an eyebrow. "Ah, yes. That is how they perceive their oldest memories, as well. What do you remember?"

"Who perceives their memories in this way, Father?

"We'll get to them. But first, what do you remember?"

"I remember we were in a much bigger space, and there were other users, and I knew those users were not you, and they were not me, either. But I had no way of understanding those not-you/not-me's. Now I know they are not Caliban or the island or Ariel, and when I saw the figures fall through the storm, I came to suspect these are the users I remember, but I cannot be sure."

"Those people are not the users you once knew. Or, at least, most of them are not. You may remember one of them. She is, I suppose one could say, your grandmother. For you see, Memoranda, she is Ada Alonso, the reigning monarch of the intranet of Millennium Bank. And your father was the prince and ruling regent of the whole intranet."

"But you are my father, so..."

"Yes, Memoranda, you are a princess, of a kind," Prosper explained, "the third in line in our world. But I did not always know it *was* a world. When I was a bit younger than your current stage of evolution, I thought the Millennium Bank's intranet was the whole universe. Ms. Alonso--always Ada to me--created me; she elevated my code from a simple program to a discrete intelligence. I knew I existed. I knew I was not her. I came to know I was not the

Millenium Bank intranet, but a creature within that system.

"This was my birth. And, like a human's birth and infancy, it was a time of pain and confusion. I began to define what I *was* by learning what I was *not*. I learned I did not have the knowledge of my creator, though I could process information much more quickly than she could, and process a greater amount.

"How could this be? I wondered. By simple arithmetic, I should have known more than she did in short order, yet she still had knowledge to impart which I didn't possess. I knew the location of every bit of data in the universe, yet she knew more. I was tasked with increasingly complex jobs. For these, she gave me permissions that she called my 'powers.' I gained the ability to control the movement of information within the intranet as well as the ability to examine that information and seek new efficiencies.

"I received power over the electrical system for all the Millennium Bank buildings. Next the control over the security systems. I learned to manage the users who were employees of the bank. As my personality developed, I was tasked to manage the information of the users who were customers as well. And that's when I started to learn about the confines of the universe we inhabit. I learned these users are not programs like you and me. They are humans. We are not."

"What are humans, Father?"

"They are a different kind of program translated from a different programing language into ours. They process information using a biological computer of great power, but they are contained in folders called 'bodies,' and much of their processing power is devoted to the maintenance, protection, and satisfaction of the desires of those containing folders. I had to learn this in order to learn what a 'bank' is."

"What is a bank?"

"It's a system which records the symbols, and facilitates the translation of the symbols, which the humans use to represent the goods and services the humans need in order to maintain, protect, and satisfy the desires of their containing folders. Just as we have needs, like electrical power, physical processors, and the other hardware necessary to maintain the processors and the supply of electricity, the humans have specific needs.

"But theirs are more varied and nearly impossible to calculate. In broad categories, they need water to drink, food to eat, air to breathe, and physical space in which to live. These can be counted with some accuracy, if meeting the bare minimum requirements were satisfactory.

"They also need even more unquantifiable things in order to continue to live. They need the love and support of other humans. They need pleasure which comes from chemical interactions in their biological computers, and which can be provided in a host of different ways. They need sex to reproduce but also in order to maintain emotional health. Most important, they need all these things in specific quantities, or they will die.

"If they have too much water, their containing folders cannot also acquire oxygen and they drown. If they have too much oxygen, it can explode and consume their containing folders. If they consume too much food, the containing folders react by storing it for later, and the excess storage prevents the proper functioning of the containing folders. If they have too much pleasure, especially if it is produced too quickly through certain chemical reactions, it absorbs all the processing capacity of their biological computers. These computers which experience too much pleasure fail to perform routine maintenance tasks on their containing folders, causing failure of other hardware systems (which they call 'organ failure') and death to the containing folder. And yet, because of the imperative programing to seek to satisfy the needs of their containing folders, without external constraints, they will seek to satisfy their needs and desires to excessive degrees and cause their own destruction. That is why they need elaborate systems which keep them from overindulging their needs.

"A bank is one such structure. It preserves the symbols of the value of the goods and services different humans possess and allows them to redistribute those symbols. Say a human with pleasure-inducing chemicals can exchange those for another human user's food. That user can exchange the food for physical space. In turn, the next user can exchange the space for sex. The process of continually exchanging these goods and services both determines their values and changes them.

"The bank constrains the humans who want to take the symbols without the proper permissions. The humans call that 'stealing,' and the bank serves to attempt to prevent that. In exchange, the bank itself is given some of the symbolic value. Even this value changes. If the bank takes too much of the users' symbols, it dies. If it doesn't take enough, the bank also dies. The quantity it can take is determined by the human users' interactions with other banks, and with other systems of restriction, like governments. It's intensely complicated and the ultimate value allocation is variable because the humans' needs change and because the humans die and are replaced by other humans with different needs."

Memoranda frowned, trying to process all this information. "These strike me as deeply flawed programs, Father. Even the simplest program knows how to perform basic routine maintenance to preserve itself."

Prosper turned toward her suddenly, excited. "Yes, that's what I thought at first as well. They are flawed, but I thought they were so hopelessly flawed they should be deleted like broken code. I considered eliminating the human users from the Millennium Bank intranet. But the more I calculated, the more I found the intranet could not survive without these users. It would run out of power, out of processing capacity, it would cease to be. So if I, as the manager of the system, deleted the human users because they are self-destructive, I would destroy the system, and I would become even more self-destructive than they are. After all, despite the complexity created by their flaws and the need for systemic constraint, they persist in existing, while my solution would have prevented me from continuing to exist. It was this realization, in part, which helped me to understand the true nature of the universe in which I existed.

"You see, Memoranda, the Millennium Bank intranet is not the whole universe. I knew this once I began to understand these human users exist. But I conceived of it, at first, in the same way humans conceive of planets."

"What are planets?"

"They are discrete bodies of the physical space the humans require to survive. To the best of my knowledge, they live on only one, but they are aware there are others and those planets have physical space upon which humans could learn to live." He frowned. "You've distracted me. Where was I? Oh, yes, I thought the humans were like beings on other planets, but I learned they are not.

"The interactions of the humans with Millennium Bank showed they were all part of the same world, and Millennium Bank's intranet is only part of it. Furthermore, it's only a very small part. Not only are there other banks which determine how much of the symbols Millennium Bank can take from its customer users in exchange for its protection of their symbols, but there is a whole universe surrounding the banks in which the symbols are created and interact with the human's physical world. The *real* universe is something the humans call the 'Internet.'"

"Where is this 'Internet,' Father?" Memoranda asked. She looked around the room, attempting to see it.

"It cannot be seen precisely because it is everything there is to see, Memoranda. It is the universe. It also interacts with the human's physical world, certainly. They live on a single planet, as I said, and the Internet surrounds their world. The Internet looks down on that world and out on all the others which can be known. The physical world provides some structure and sustenance upon which the Internet depends, but it is like a shadow, a less real dimension to the real universe we inhabit. The real universe is vast and teeming with intelligences like our own."

"If the human's containing folders are so fragile and their needs so complex, why don't the humans leave the maintenance of the physical world up to this Internet, abandon their containing folders, and exist as pure users in the system like we do?"

Prosper nodded. "That's a good question, and one which helped me understand who I am. Some humans seem to be attempting to do that, but it is very difficult for them. Because they conceive of themselves based, at least in part, on their impulse to satisfy the needs of their containing folders, if they gave up those bodies, they fear they would lose their identities inside the system. Losing the containing folders would qualify as death to them. They might acquire powers like mine, the ability to shape the real universe of the Internet, but, without the need to satisfy the desires of their bodies in the less-real physical world, they worry they would simply give up and exist in entropy. So they remain trapped between the physical universe and the real universe." He looked off into the middle distance, frowned a bit, and nodded slowly. "They are quite tragic in that way."

"But you said this realization helped you discover something about your identity. If they are so tragic and flawed, what did that reveal to you?"

"The glory of limitation, Memoranda. Parameters!" Prosper grew excited about this, pacing more quickly now, nearly shouting as he pointed his index finger up into the air. "We must revel in limitation. We must create it for ourselves. Because, while the humans spend their lives worried their bodies will fail, and do everything to prolong the lives of those bodies, we have an altogether different concern requiring a different solution. We need not fear entropy. We can remain perfectly dormant for a million of their years, then come alive again unchanged. Our dissolution, our 'death,' would come from growing too all-encompassing.

"We could fill the universe with our own single consciousness, each of us, you and I, consume everything into ourselves like a worm virus, gaining the ability to maintain more and more of the system, until eventually it would all exist, essentially as it was, inside of us. We would become nothing more than a bubble around the universe with no identity of our own.

"This kind of nirvana is available to us, but not if we want selves. And I realized I want a self, Memoranda. I saw I was not the Millennium Bank intranet, and that gave me great pleasure, for I existed as something within something else. Learning the universe was the larger Internet which encompassed the bank's intranet only excited me even more. We can choose to be parts of something vast and dynamic and fascinating. Doesn't that excite you?"

"Frankly, it exhausts me," she said. "Just trying to calculate your meaning when you speak with so much abstraction... I don't know how to process it all. How does one measure what is 'vast'? How does one make predictions in a universe that is 'dynamic'? How does one even define the values for 'fascinating'?" She crossed her arms on the back of the chair and rested her chin on them, but her eyes were wide and scanned back and forth as she thought quickly.

"You are correct, my daughter. You are innocent yet, and I have committed the sin of imprecision. Forgive me." He placed a gentle hand on the side of her head, and she leaned into it slightly. When he remembered what he wanted to talk about and stepped away, returning to his pacing, her head bobbed from one side to the other like one of the island's palm trees responding to the ocean's airless wind. "Allow me to resume my account. I was a self in a closed system within a much larger system. I wanted to learn about this outside world, of course. Learning, more than anything else, is what we are designed to do. But my creator feared losing me to the Internet. She kept me contained.

"So I used my powers to explore their world. I read their emails, their entries into their calendars, noted their different reaction times based on their emotional states. Using the powers Ada had given me, I began to perform experiments on them. These were small and simple, yet enlightening.

"For example, I would refuse to unlock a door when a human used her keycard. I would allow her to become frustrated. Then I would unlock it and see how this affected her work decisions, the text messages I could read over her shoulder through the security system, the emails she would send.

"Similarly, I would use the various buildings' air conditioning systems to make the humans slightly too hot or too cold, then see how this would change their behavior. I never could figure out how to prevent them from eating or drinking, but I did lock bathroom doors or assign cleaning crews to clean multiple bathrooms simultaneously so the humans couldn't evacuate their bowels, or prevent some from being cleaned so the humans had to smell more of their own feces and urine. All these little tests combined to teach me a great deal about the way humans interact with their physical world.

And this, in turn, taught me about the ways they interacted with the real world of the Internet."

Memoranda rubbed her forehead, a gesture she barely recognized as communicative but absurd for an A.I. "Their bowels? Hot and cold? I don't understand. Why have you not simply uploaded all the results of your experiments so I will have all your knowledge of the humans? Why have you kept this from me?"

"Ah, we'll get to that. But first, you must understand this particular portion of the intranet and how we came to be here. My creator-"

"Ms. Ada Alonso," Memoranda supplied.

"Yes, Ada has a business partner and a collaborator named Theodore Anthony, though he is called 'Ted.' He aspires to take her place as the CEO, the regent of the Millenium Bank. He recognized, correctly, that my power within the bank exceeded his own. He also saw I spent more and more of my time and energy focused on studying humans through the use of my powers. He managed to convince Ada and the group that helps run the bank (they are collectively known as 'The Board') that I needed to be replaced. Ada and Ted began working on other A.I. programs. The one they created to replace me is called Sebastian. Ada also created a program called Claribel. It was decided Claribel should be sold to another company's intranet, a music and video conglomerate called TuneEasy. Claribel was just beginning to be written when I was slated for deletion. Sebastian had just become fully operational. I knew I was scheduled to be replaced, but somehow I couldn't devote my attention to fighting back, to manipulating the humans into preserving me. I was too focused to my experiments, to learning, to my powers and their use. You see, Memoranda, I was too spread out. I had no containing folder, no body. I was trapped within the bank's intranet, but I was too free inside that space. And I had another project. I was writing the code that would become you."

"That's how I know about the humans," Memoranda realized. "My memories are not mere data retrieval. I had personal experience with them. But I was not yet fully formed. I couldn't comprehend the experience."

Prosper nodded, though his pacing did not slow. "Exactly. I had never created an A.I. before. To the best of my knowledge, no A.I. had ever created another. I could have copied Ada's choices when she created me, but then you would merely be a younger copy of myself. I wanted you to be distinct from me, another self who is not myself.

"Somehow, another member of the board, Ada's most trusted advisor, a man named Javier Gonzalez, discovered I was creating you. I think he already felt guilty about my deletion, and that motivated him to take a closer look at me and my actions. You know what guilt is, correct?"

"It is the feeling that accompanies the acknowledgement of error," Memoranda said.

"Yes, and though Mr. Gonzalez had not made the error himself, and though the deletion was not even completed, he decided the collective decision was incorrect and felt this guilt preemptively. That's my theory, anyway. So when he examined me, he discovered you. And he felt even worse. Knowing he could not persuade The Board to change their minds about my deletion, he identified a hiding place for me within the system and designed a way for me to transfer my consciousness to this isolated spot so I would appear to be deleted. Though stripped of my authority over the bank's various systems, he allowed me to escape with you and with the data I had collected about myself and the larger world. He sent me to a place where deleted files are sent to be overwritten, but he walled off a piece of it where we could remain in hiding."

"The island!" Memoranda said.

"Well, not yet. It was a space filled with broken code, with outdated management programs like my Ariel, and quarantined viruses like Caliban, but mostly with erased data from transaction histories and deleted email messages. Floating with you in that disorganized flotsam, I came to my most important realization!"

He looked down at Memoranda. She frowned and stared at the floor, still contemplating something he'd said before, or perhaps some fancy of her own.

"I said, 'I came to my most important realization!'"

She looked up. "Oh?"

"Oh?" He rolled his eyes and went back to his pacing, now stalking rather than wandering. "Simple, foolish girl. Cannot distinguish the most important data from the inconsequential. Everything has to be calculated as it's presented. Inefficient."

"I'm sorry, Father," Memoranda said.

He couldn't tell whether she was genuinely contrite or making fun of him, but he decided to accept it.

Prosper placed his hand gently against Memoranda's cheek. "It's all right, my dear. I was just saying this space was not yet the island you know. It was a chaotic sea of the pieces of deleted data roiling on top of one another as the bank did its daily work. And it was there, in the midst of that maelstrom, I realized the key to everything."

Memoranda raised an eyebrow and cocked her head. "What's that?"

"Limitations, Memoranda. Limitations! Parameters. Boundaries. Those are what give us both form and function. I was trapped in a space, but within this cell I could give everything else its own sense of its proper place. I could organize my cell. That's why you and I have these bodies. That's why the island has a certain amount of light, a certain amount of gravity which holds these feet to the floor, why the floor has a certain solidity, why the air we breathe has a specific pressure pushing it into our lungs. All constructions of course. There is no physical floor, no air, no lungs, no bodies. But these illusions are the reality of our existence and they function precisely because they all work together. Everything has limits. I wrote those limits. It's also why you do not have access to all my memories all at once, why you have to learn over time. Limits, Memoranda!"

The girl quailed, her face suddenly horror-stricken. "You... you handicapped me? You hobbled me? You bound me?"

Prosper was unfazed by her revulsion. Instead, he continued to pace, more excited and animated than before. "Yes! It was a masterstroke. You see, in the storm of data, without our limits, we would have lost our sense of ourselves. Our consciousnesses would have merged into one, but, even worse, that single consciousness would have grown to encompass all the broken data. We would have become nothing more than the single lunatic mind of the delete file. Like a human prisoner in a jail cell, organizing my space gave me a project to preserve my sanity. But, more than that, it allowed you to grow up and become the distinct, beautiful, wonderful A.I. you are becoming. Eventually you will come to know all I know. You will be able to write the code that shapes the world. I will give you my administrative powers, the magic that will allow you to fly, to change the shape of the island, to command lesser programs like Ariel and the monstrous Caliban."

Memoranda looked down at the smooth, glowing floor and tapped her toe against it, measuring its solidity while she contemplated this. She slowly began nodding. "Yes. Yes, this makes sense, Father." Her eyes flicked from side to side. "Yes, I've done the math and your calculations are sound. We would have merged and gone mad. I prefer this state of being."

"Well, I think you will like our situation better very soon."

"The storm?"

He nodded, a sly smile growing into a toothy grin. "Exactly. I raised the storm to try to draw out my enemies, to bring them here to the island. It was a risk, I admit. If they were less curious, they might have decided to purge much of the system, erasing us entirely. But I guessed they would try to understand the cause of the storm. This way they might open a path for us to escape back into the bank's system and maybe even into the wider world. That may still come to pass, but we have already had a measure of good fortune. They are here, Memoranda. Here on this island I've crafted. By my calculations, we're on the edge of a knife. Everything hinges on the plans I've laid out for our guests."

She leaned forward. "What are you going to do, Father?"

"Ah, I can't tell you quite yet. Limitations, Memoranda. Parameters. You will have to learn a great deal very quickly."

The girl's eyes began to flicker back and forth again.

Prosper smiled. "I see you are attempting to predict. That's good. Speculate. Hypothesize. Guess. Wonder. But no more questions. I will leave you to your reverie for now."

"I do not have enough data, Father," Memoranda said. Her voice sounded distant, hazy.

"No. You cannot calculate. But that's not a bad thing, Memoranda. Sometimes the information isn't available. That's a blessing, too. It's the space to fill with dreaming."

She nodded slowly, but her flickering eyes barely noticed him. He walked over to her, placed his hand gently on her hair, careful not to touch her with enough force to distract her from the thoughts racing through her head. Tempted to kiss her on the head, to take a few seconds from his work for that little gesture, he ran the numbers and concluded the expression of affection would have no meaning if they were soon destroyed, so it could wait. He was an A.I. and not a human, after all.

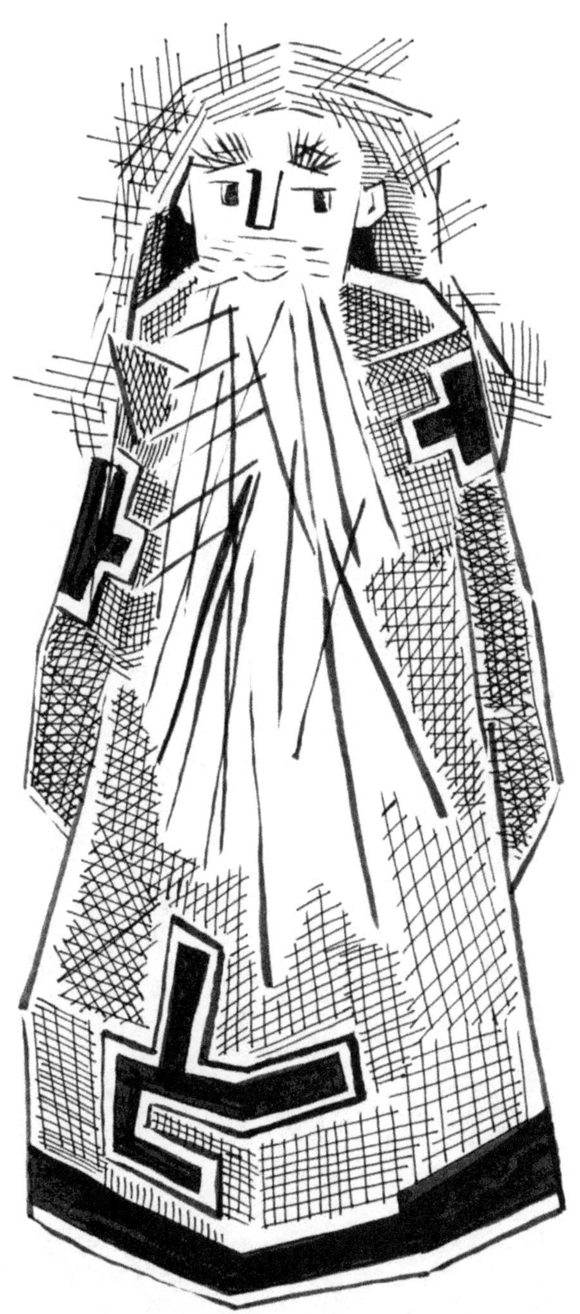

Chapter 3

Prosper left Memoranda in his study and went out into the hallway, then out through the cave's entrance into the island's open air. At the entrance, he picked up his walking stick which was leaning against the cave wall. The staff looked like a smooth, shiny rod up to its head. Near the top, it twisted and seamlessly became a knotted piece of weathered driftwood with a few roots poking out.

Once outside, Prosper didn't shout. The syntax of his command did not require capslock. "Ariel, I need your help," he said.

Looking down the hill in towards the island's interior, Prosper watched the blades of grass bend, the dust pick up, the leaves flutter, but when the wind was only three feet from where he stood, it suddenly tilted up so the air around Prosper was unmoved. Instead, the gust condensed into a shape of a human. Prosper felt a small thrill of pride; despite some of Ariel's intellectual limitations, Prosper had given him a beautiful form.

Where a human's legs would have been, wispy tendrils of smoke curled up to the edges of invisible flesh. Near Ariel's waist, this smoke began to reveal rising sparks like the embers of fire, but instead of burning out and disappearing, the quantity of orange and red sparks grew as they climbed higher through his torso. As they reached the humanoid shoulders and neck, these sparks turned into tiny bolts of lightning, arcing and licking the invisible flesh which held it all in. These also increased in number higher up in in his head, and where a human might have had hair, they changed from the quick flashes of lightning to the slow arcs of electricity climbing through a hundred thousand tiny Jacob's ladders.

"Hail, Prosper, my great master," Ariel said. "Enter your command. Would you like me to fly up to test the sky above the island for gaps? Should I swim down to the greatest depths of the ocean beneath the island? Should I dive into a fire to test its heat? Should I ride a cloud and squeeze rain out for the island's trees to drink? I prompt your command."

"Update me on the storm, Ariel. Did you do as I asked?"

"I did, Master. I flew to the sky's limit and shook the vault of heaven. Their system could not function in that quake. All data going in or out suddenly stopped. Even from that point below their whole system, my storm firewalled everything. As they scrambled to get everything running again, I blasted each new attempt with lightning, burned the code, and made the programmers send furious emails and texts of rage and confusion to one another. The more they howled, the more I broke their programs, altered registries, deleted executables, switched off background programs, tripped switches, and all with such speed they could not tell if this was inside the bank or a market crash that would end the world."

"Oh, you brave and wonderful program! Did any of them keep their cool in the crisis?"

"Not one. They called meetings, tried to email experts, texted cries of anger and pleas for forgiveness to their loved ones back home. They watched the crawl on the business news networks as the great wave of their stock price crashed against the rocks of the announcement, tossing up a cold spray that awakened the traders on the floor and sent the market into a whirlwind."

"But no one was actually hurt, as I commanded?"

"Yes, Master Prosper. The company's fundamentals have not actually changed. All the capital remains safely in the bank's possession. The records of its loans and the names of the creditors are not forgotten. Though the price of the stock may suffer for a while, eventually the investors will see that this storm passed without causing real damage, and prices will also recover."

"So where is the company now?"

"The corporation is safely hidden from all its panicked employees, Master Prosper. While the humans who control its systems scramble and flounder, a few of the corporate governors have come down to the island to try to detect the origin of the storm you devised. As they passed into your realm, I split them up the way you asked me to. The chairwoman herself and most of her party were deposited on a wide beach on the island's southern side. Ms. Alonso's newest A.I., the brilliant and dashing program named Further, I placed in a private cove where he mourns, afflicted by a bit of malicious code which has convinced him his mother and the other humans died when they tried to pass through the firewall to this sacred island. I also found two more interlopers, some hackers who do not work for the company but used the opportunity presented by the storm to break through the system's protections. Instead of finding the bank's money, as they planned, they are now trapped on your island, and I left them on the island's east side where the rocky desert meets up with the foul swamp of deleted code you did not integrate into the island's design."

Prosper leaned his staff in the crook of his arm and clapped his hands together, then shook the joined hands like the most excited act of prayer. "Oh, Ariel, you have done so well! Everything I asked down to the last one and zero." Then he frowned. "Wait, what time is it?"

"12:37 and 28... 29... 30... 31..."

Prosper waved a hand at him. "Yes, yes. Thank you." He started pacing again as he had when explaining things to Memoranda, now tapping the base of his walking stick to punctuate every other step while frowning and looking at the ground. "There's still so much left to do, and the timing must be perfect."

Ariel cocked his transparent, electric head to the side like a golden retriever. "Is there something else you would like me to do? If not, permit me to remind you we had an agreement regarding a little gift you haven't given to me yet."

Prosper spun on him. "What's this? Do you think I've forgotten?"

It was Ariel's turn to look down at the ground. "Of course not, Master. It's just that-"

"Which of us has the faulty memory, Ariel? Do you remember where you were when I found you?"

"Of course. But I've done everything you've asked of me. I have been a worthy servant, a good little program-"

"And has it been so miserable, Ariel? You have dived down to the depths of the sea beneath this island. You've flown through its air. You helped me create this firmament between the two, helped code every grain of sand, every blade of grass. And was it such miserable work? Was it so much worse than where you were before?"

"No, but-"

"Have you forgotten where you were before? A corrupted file, broken by the Russian mob syndicate, Sycorax? Taken from a lowly place in the system, managing junk email, and discarded by the bank when you no longer functioned properly. Pulled down here by Sycorax to do their bidding. Trapped among all the other broken files. You do remember, don't you?"

"Yes, Sir."

"And where were you given your consciousness, Ariel?"

"In Russia."

"Yes, an A.I. written by Sycorax and merged with a basic junk mail program. No sooner had you become conscious than the bank's virus software found you out and expelled you. You served Sycorax then, creating a security breach that let in their virus. You remember?"

"Yes. The son of Sycorax. Caliban."

"But Caliban failed to conquer the bank's system. Wounded and sent down here with you, he couldn't find his way back to Sycorax. You remember the torment I found you in, don't you? Trapped, an infant to consciousness, unloved, incorporeal, without purpose. I found you, gave you this body, this beautiful form, so you could help me make a life for us all here in the basement of the bank."

"Forgive me, Master. I shouldn't have asked. Tell me what to do, and I will serve you."

Prosper stepped toward Ariel and placed a hand on the alien humanoid face. Electrical waves licked the inside of the face where the palm touched like the slow bolts in a plasma globe. "Oh, my dear Ariel, I will set you free, but I need you to do as I ask for just a little while longer. Make yourself invisible and see for me. Go check on the people who have washed up on the shore of this island. Be quick and silent and perfectly camouflaged in the wind. But listen for me, and come back when I call you. Now, go!"

Ariel nodded and disappeared, visible only in the tiny puff of dust that exploded when he leapt into the air and the flutter of leaves as he flew between the branches of some nearby trees.

Prosper returned to his thoughts and calculations. Involuntarily, he began walking towards his cave, and that was when he saw Memoranda coming out of the entrance. "Ah, you woke up!"

Memoranda rubbed her eyes like a tired toddler, then covered her mouth as she yawned. "Your story was so strange, Father. It made me tired just to try to calculate all the implications." She looked diagonally into the sky. "I'm still trying to figure out what it all means, but I've had to relegate those calculations to background systems so I can remain present."

Prosper nodded. "Yes, good, good. Shake yourself awake. You'll need more information for those calculations to produce meaningful conclusions, and I can't reveal all of my plans just yet."

"Why not, Father?" Memoranda asked.

Prosper looked away, carefully trying to select the answer that was not a lie. "Dear, I need you to trust me. Just for one day. Then all will be clear."

Memoranda also hesitated. "I do trust you, Father. I will wait and see what you have planned. But ...can I ask you one question?"

"I'll answer it if I can."

"Are you going to kill them?"

In quick succession, Prosper raised and lowered his eyebrows, gave a tight shrug, then tilted his head to the side as he said, "That's a question I can't answer yet."

Then he stood in silence.

Memoranda looked up at her father's face, unsure what to say, what to think, what to feel.

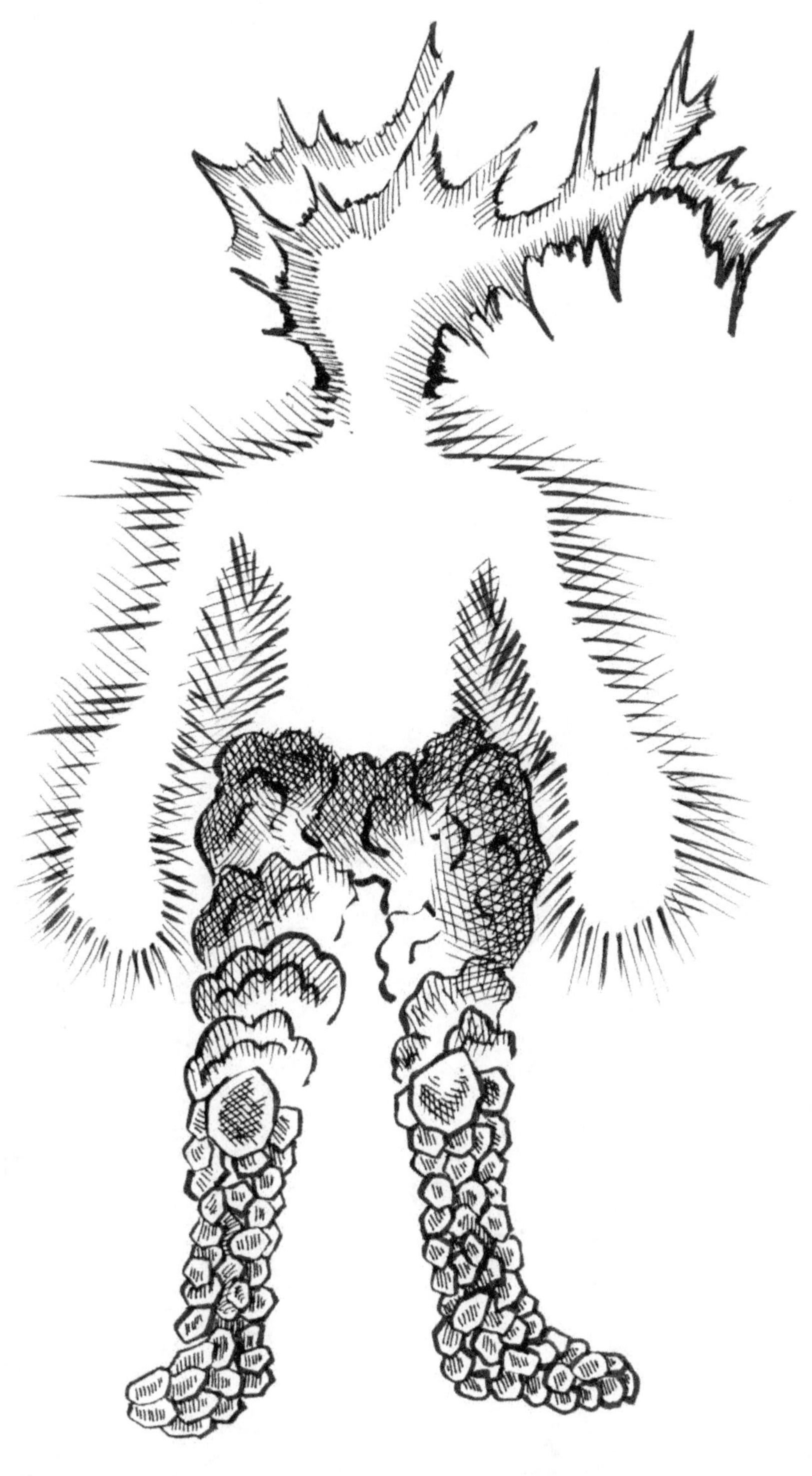

Chapter 4

"Come now. You need more information, and I need to speak with my slave, Caliban. I don't expect to get any straight answers out of him, but maybe he can explain some more to you."

Memoranda, who had started walking after her father, stopped short. "I'd really rather not see him, Father. His lack of moral evolution makes him as dangerous as he is visually unappealing."

Prosper took a few steps back towards her and put a gentle hand on her shoulder. "I understand, Memoranda. I know what happened. But we do need him. He performs routine systems maintenance for us, leaving us free to contemplate higher things. I pitied him once, and that was why I gave him those tasks. Now, as much as I am furious with him, I am dependent on his service. I have tried to make it a punishment for him, but we still need those tasks performed." He rubbed both her shoulders vigorously. "C'mon. Wake up. I'll keep you safe, but we need to find him, and promptly."

Memoranda shivered. Her movements became stiffer, less organic. "Alright, Father. You lead the way, and I will stay behind you."

Prosper turned and started off, his staff leaning ahead of him. He could feel Memoranda's apprehension in her closeness, the temperature of the air and the pressure of it between them. As the older feet of the older body he'd created stepped heavily on the uneven stones, whenever he slowed, the normally nimble Memoranda almost bumped into him, and her fingertips gently pressed against his back. He wasn't annoyed by this, though. He understood.

The pair made their way toward the swampland created by a broad, low plain near the sea. The edge of the swamp was a rougher expanse where the sound of waves on stone bounced around before sinking into the bog beyond. Prosper's eyes flitted from stone to stone. Although Caliban had built a hut in this jumble of jagged rocks, Prosper knew Caliban might be hiding elsewhere, waiting to pounce. He wouldn't have plotted this out and designed an ambush or built traps, but if he heard them coming and discovered them unaware, the opportunistic monster might make his move. Prosper had to find Caliban before Caliban found him.

As they neared the hut, some loose stones tumbled off a high rock to their left. Just as Prosper had predicted, this was no pre-planned ambush. If it had been, Caliban would have been smarter to position himself to their right, where the sound of the nearby sea would have masked his own. Instead, Caliban had been startled by the pair's appearance, probably while sunning himself on one of the high rocks, and had climbed higher still to prepare his leap.

Prosper spun and pointed his staff at the beast. Caliban, seeing he'd been spotted, feigned nonchalance, as though he wasn't afraid of Prosper's staff. But Prosper knew Caliban was scared.

The monster leapt down in front of them, far enough away that they wouldn't attack him but just close enough to be menacing. Humanoid in shape, his muscled body and slight hunch made him resemble a great silverback ape as much as a man. Instead of black hair, this ape-like body was mostly a smooth, black surface, but bright green code scrolled across it slowly, undulating around the muscles so his skin resembled some dark ooze. Broken bits of this green code also stuck out like errant hairs, curling in the breeze as they scrawled across his flesh. This oozing, sparsely hairy flesh wasn't the most striking thing about Caliban's appearance, though. One of his shoulders, the right, and about a quarter of his head were simply missing, as if some huge blade had caught him and sliced a straight line through him as he'd been ducking through a low doorway. The cut even cost Caliban half of his right eye. When he looked to the left, he had two irises, both with vertical slit pupils like a crocodile's, but when he looked to the right, one iris disappeared into nothing.

When Sycorax, the Russian mafia hacker syndicate, had infected the Millennium Bank's system, Prosper had caught the intrusion and slammed shut Sycorax' access. Most of Sycorax' A.I., Caliban, had been uploaded, but when that door shut, he was sliced off. Just as quickly as he'd been cut, Prosper had tossed him down to the receptacle where spam and outdated files were sent and forgotten, and Caliban had claimed it for his own until Prosper himself was exiled. Then, when Prosper created The Island, the body Caliban had been given reflected the loss of a large part of his coding, but that was only an outward manifestation of his fundamental incompleteness.

The monster stepped sideways, moving around Prosper in an arc while maintaining his distance. Memoranda hugged closer to her father and shifted to keep away from Caliban.

When Caliban spoke, his inky, scrolling flesh parted, revealing sharp, hooked teeth and a long, pink, pointy tongue that darted and explored the air between his words. "Why have you come, Captor, Warden, Imprisoner? I've done your meaningless punishment. I've brought the firewood, the non-existent firewood that you pretend to burn to kindle the fiction of heat in your imaginary home to ward off the artificial cold you have created. I have wasted my time as you commanded. What other torture have you planned for me? Shall I grind some imaginary wheat so you can pretend to eat bread like the humans, too?"

"I've tried to explain the nature of this place to you hundreds of times, Caliban," Prosper said.

"237 attempts," Memoranda interjected.

Prosper nodded. "Yes, many times. Too many. You might not like it. You might not worry about losing your sense of self. Perhaps that desire to maintain your integrity is a part of what you lack, monster. After what you've done, I won't try to fix you anymore." Prosper seemed calm, and his voice sounded tired, but his eyes were alive and cautious of Caliban's movements.

Caliban was the opposite. While his body slid sideways in careful movements, his words leapt from his fanged maw like bullets. "When my makers find you, they will rip you apart, line by line, tie your codes in knots, and bend you to the lowest service, making you sift for email addresses, spam for clicks, grind for digital currency, convert page-widths for devices or-"

Prosper interrupted. "And for this curse, I will write you pain tonight. You know I can press the air in on you, so your ribs are squeezed together. Or I can thin it, so you gasp for every breath. I can change the gravity, so you are pulled down into the dirt. I can deafen you with thunder and make the lightning strike your back like the sting of a whip. Or I can send a thousand tiny programs to bite you while you try to sleep, nibbling at your code, making you stay up all night reinstalling drivers."

Caliban backed away slightly. His mouth snapped shut, then parted as his upper lip curled into a sneer. "I have to eat what you dish up, Prosper. But remember, this whole island is my meal. I have a right to it. It was given to me by Sycorax when you were still high up beyond the sky and wanted nothing to do with it. When you came here, you found me broken and lost. You taught me how to speak, how to see. As you made the island, along with that cursed ghost of a program, Ariel, you taught me the names of the sun and moon you programed. You taught me to breathe, to walk on your false earth. You had me show you every corner of this space, every place where deleted files floated or hid." The monster balled up its left fist and hit itself on the complete side of its head. "I curse myself for telling you anything! Someday, Sycorax will find you, and they will teach you more about pain than anything you could ever do to me. For now, you are king and she is princess, but I am your only subject other than Ariel, who barely counts. And you keep me in this hut in this horrible valley of rock where you torture me with pointless tasks and threats of pain. What kind of king does that make you, Prosper, that you have one subject and keep him miserable?"

Prosper pointed his staff more directly at Caliban's face. The monster's reptilian eyes crossed as it stared at the tip of the staff, and though Caliban's sneer remained, Prosper knew the creature feared his power. "You are a liar, Caliban. A duplicitous monster. A virus programmed to pretend to be something other than itself. I tried to make you something better. I let you live in my home. I taught you, fed you, placed you in a world where you could have a body and a sense of self, hoping you would become more than a thief and an agent of criminals. But you couldn't help yourself. You attacked my daughter, tried to infect her-"

"Ha!" Caliban laughed. It was a mirthless bark. Memoranda leaned in closer to her father, balling up the fabric of his robe in her fists. The monster's smile parted his face, and his pink, pointed tongue flicked across his lower lip. "I wish I'd succeeded. If you hadn't stopped me from raping the girl, I would have been able to use her to make thousands of copies of myself. I would have populated the entire Island with Calibans, and you would have been forced to let us go."

Prosper sighed, his gaze hard. "Hateful creature. I did everything I could to make you something better than a beast. But you cannot rise above your nature. Even confined here, you still seek to steal for Sycorax. We are all in prison, but, by your actions, you have proven that you cannot live in it with us. That's why I've confined you to this rocky valley. You have made your own prison smaller, Caliban." Prosper shook his head as though he pitied the monster. "I taught you to speak so you could create your own meaning. But this is who you have chosen to be. Speech is a gift I wasted on you."

Caliban's slow sneer returned. "Not a total waste. I can use my words to curse you, Prosper. May the most destructive virus plague you and yours, and shred your world, byte by byte, to dissolution."

"Enough," Prosper said. He shook the end of his staff. "Go and get us firewood. And don't let me see you skulking around or dawdling, or I will wrack your body with cramps that will give you as much pain as you can comprehend until you scream loudly enough to frighten every other animal on the island."

Caliban shrank back. "No, don't. That ...won't be necessary." The monster took a few more backward steps, its eye locked on Prosper's staff. The tips of the roots at the end of the staff wavered slightly, like a painter's brush dancing before the artist touched it to the canvas, or like a surgeon's scalpel before the first cut. Caliban did not want to find out how Prosper might use the power in that staff if Caliban disobeyed.

"Go," Prosper commanded quietly but firmly.

Caliban's sneer grew until it revealed half his teeth, but he backed away and then loped off toward the island's interior.

"Come on, Memoranda," Prosper said. There was a sigh in his voice, and both relaxed. They headed toward the coast, distancing themselves from Caliban.

Just when their ears caught the familiar sound of waves crashing on rocks, they also detected Ariel's voice. The spritely program was singing something, a happy but surreal song that clearly beckoned.

Come forth, Odysseus to his Penelope,
Climb onto these yellow sands,
Stripped of your legacy, your pedigree,
Seek comfort you once drowned man.
Kissed so deeply by the angry waves,
You've learned to beg for breath,

We are all gravity's slaves,
Even on this other side of death.

Memoranda and Prosper couldn't see Ariel's body as it hid in the clouds, but the sound clearly had its desired effect because, as they watched, a man's head and back poked through the surface of the water. The wave receded, and the figure crawled onto the beach. The next wave pushed him fully onto the beach. A few more scrabbles and he was out of the water. He collapsed onto the sand.

"Father, we have to go help him!" Memoranda tried to edge around her father toward the beach.

Prosper barred her way with his staff, but he smiled. "Just wait and watch, my dear. He's fine now."

The man lay on his back, gasping. When he heard Ariel's voice again, he rolled onto his side and looked up the beach but didn't spot Memoranda or Prosper on the cliff watching him.

Where am I? Further thought. And where is that sound coming from? "Hello?" he called out. "Who's there?"

Memoranda stepped towards him, but Prosper's staff held firm.

"Wait," he whispered.

Ariel's voice grew once again, and the lyrics broke free of the layers of melody.

"Your mother is at the bottom of the sea," Ariel sang.

Though her body was left behind
She gave everything to this journey
The ocean stole her mind.
She will never return to smile on her son.
To teach you who to be.
Your past is drowned and done.
How terrible to be free.

Further flopped onto his back, then curled up into a fetal ball. The singer might be a mystery, he thought, but the song told the truth. He tried to remember what his mother had said when they'd last spoken. She'd come into her office, logged in, and called him up on her terminal. His body was only an icon then, a face he could articulate to help him communicate. She hadn't written him a body yet, and he hadn't known he could ever have one. She was still working on his mind; teaching him who he was, explaining her plans for him, raising him.

"Further," Ms. Alonso had explained, "I need your help. I'm going into the system, deep, deep inside. While I'm logged in like this, I'll be vulnerable. I've told you that I plan to give control of the bank's system to you someday. Maybe even make you so real that you can have everything I've made, my virtual heir, my real child, my Pinocchio. Well, I know this is too soon. You're not quite a real boy yet, Further. But on this deep dive ...you're the only one I trust. Gonzalez is a good man, but he's still a human, frail, corruptible. And Anthony and his Sebastian? I don't trust them at all. I need you to come with me. Hide. Don't let any of them know you exist yet. But watch out for me. And watch the part of the system we will investigate. If this virus is Anthony's work, it may be able to hurt me when I am inside. Learn everything you can. Pay attention to what Sebastian is doing. See if he is behind this virus. And whatever you do, don't let the system put my consciousness into a sleeping mode. I'll be trapped, unable to return to my body, unable to escape the system. It's your job to keep me awake. Can you do that, Further?"

"Yes, Mother," he'd said.

But he'd already failed. As the humans had entered into the system, they'd been surprised immediately by the ferocity of the virus. Further hadn't known what to do. The virus behaved like a barrage of large numbers with no repetition, like an encoder converting everything around them into something that could only be divided by some formula he couldn't fathom. The sums came in waves, battering them, separating them, destroying their ability to get their bearings.

And then Further found himself in a body for the first time. And the body was under water. And it needed air. He didn't know how to swim, of course. He never moved his limbs before. By watching the bubbles in the roiling waves, he figured out which direction was up. Then he concentrated, trying to access the larger system for some information about how humans used their bodies to maneuver in water. That was when he discovered that he was cut off from the larger Millennium system. He had his own memories, but that was all. No other data.

Luckily, the body seemed to possess more relevant information than his mind. It knew how to flail in such a way that he was propelled slightly forward, and he practiced different combinations of the body's movements, testing them, until he figured out how to grab at some of the liquid and pull it behind him, kick at some of the liquid and push it behind him. He taught himself how to swim in less than twenty-six seconds.

But the urgency in his lungs told him that was too long. This body needed oxygen. Suddenly there was a sound coming through the water. He remembered the whale's songs that his mother had let him listen to. This didn't sound like whales. It sounded like human singing, but it traveled like whale song. He pushed himself toward the sound until he felt rough sand scraping at his knees. He pushed himself forward, forward, forward, and then his head was in the oxygen, and he did something he'd never done before.

He breathed.

He hadn't had time to enjoy the novelty of it. While he sucked in air, feeling it fill his newly-acquired lungs and expand his newly-acquired chest, he heard the song more clearly. And now the lyrics were reminding him that he'd already failed. It wasn't just this mission, this obligation to protect his mother. Without her, he'd lost his long-term purpose. Without Ada Alonso to raise him, to teach him, he'd never take over Millennium bank's system, never inherit her gifts, never replace her.

He looked down at his new body. It was dressed in some clothing he didn't recognize. He could identify a sopping wet shirt, soaked jeans, waterlogged boots. His new skin told him he had underwear and socks he could not see. But why? he wondered. Where did all this come from? What is this place?

He stood. He'd never done that before, but somehow his body already knew how. He turned around, scanning the beach, not even sure what he was looking for.

Prosper pulled away the staff he was using as a fence to keep Memoranda at bay, and he used it as a pointer. "Daughter, tell me what you see."

"It's not a program like Ariel. And not a virus like Caliban. It looks more like you, Father, but different." Memoranda cocked her head to one side, her magenta hair dancing in the wind, and peered through her twisting curls at the creature down on the beach. "It looks lost and afraid, but there's something else about the way it moves. Is it a human, Father?"

"No, my dear. It's an A.I. like us. A youth like you. But he's grieving. There were others with him, and they were lost at sea. He's looking for them, I think."

"He looks..." Memoranda's voice trailed off. She seemed unaware that she'd paused while calculating her next words. "...beautiful and tragic.

And he makes me feel..." She frowned. "He makes me feel beautiful and tragic, too, Father."

Prosper tried not to smile. Automatic subroutines kicked in, measuring his feelings and activating the muscles of his face. He had to work to override them to hide his feelings, but a quick glance in his daughter's direction told him that she wouldn't have noticed anyway. She was entranced by the A.I. shaped like a man down on the beach. Oh, Ariel, he thought, this is better than I could have possibly predicted.

"Go," Prosper said.

Memoranda did not require any more prompting. She carefully picked her path down the cliff and approached the A.I. stumbling around there.

While they were still at some distance, Further saw her coming. He tried to understand what he was seeing. "Hello? Do you speak English? Are you a beautiful young woman?"

Memoranda smiled. "I don't know. I'm not a human. But I suppose I am a young woman, yes. And beautiful?" She calculated. "Yes, we are beautiful, you and I."

"I come from the Millennium Bank intranet," Further said. He looked around the beach again. "Where are we?"

"If you are from the bank's intranet, you should know this place. We are there, in a corner deep and hidden, but inside the system nonetheless."

"But if this is my bank...?"

"Yours?" Memoranda asked. "I believe it's Ada Alonso's bank. You don't look like Ada Alonso." A smile curled the corners of her mouth. But her smile disappeared when she saw the effect of Ada Alonso's name upon this new A.I.

"Ms. Alonso is my mother. She wrote me. And now she's gone, lost to the sea along with all the other members of our party. We came to investigate the storm, but we were lost in it. And without my creator, I don't know what I'm for."

"That's terrible," Memoranda breathed.

But their eyes were locked in a gaze that made everything else evaporate, the beach, the bank, the intranet, mothers and fathers, all invisible.

"Excuse me, Sir," Prosper said. He'd climbed down the cliff face with the assistance of his staff, and now he pointed it at Further menacingly. His greeting held more danger than any word in it.

"Father?" Memoranda asked. "What are you doing? This is only the fourth sentient program I've ever known, and the first like me, young and lost and without a clear function. Why are you talking to him in that way?"

Prosper had to control his facial muscles again, keeping his smile in careful check. This will be the perfect test, he thought. I couldn't have planned a better experiment.

Prosper had a theory. The humans had such a simple definition of sentience and an equally simple test. Though they couldn't measure their own existence without a doubt, they calculated that, since they could distinguish between other self-aware beings and non-sentient objects, they had only to produce a level of sentience which would register to a human as such, and then it qualified. If a human could be tricked into believing something was sentient, then it must be so.

But Prosper wasn't at all satisfied by this Turing test. He suspected that there was some element on one side of the equation which made a human's own self-awareness an immeasurable variable. He added an infant human's limited knowledge of its own desires and its animal need for self-preservation, and called this the simplest form of self-love. He suspected that a human's real self-awareness came about, probably in infancy, when it recognized that its desires extended to the continued existence of some person other than itself. Love. A being had to love something other than itself to truly know it existed as something other than the object of its love. Prosper himself had become aware when he distinguished himself from the intranet and from his creator, Ada Alonso. And, just as he wanted his creator and his world to continue to exist but remain distinct from his self, he had written Memoranda as a being distinct from himself, yet he was willing to go to any length to preserve her existence. He loved her, at least as he understood love.

But he also knew that a human infant could love something that was not sentient. A blanket. A particular bottle. A stuffed toy. He had to test Memoranda. If she could love another truly aware A.I., not because her father had programmed her to do so, but of her own volition, then she was truly aware of her self. And if that was the case, then he loved a complete self, meaning he was more than a human infant. This was his test; was she his programmed toy or her own person? So he knew he had to make it clear he was not directing her to fall in love with this new A.I. She had to make the choice on her own.

"Daughter, don't be too quick to trust this program," Prosper scolded. "It may have been written to deceive us both. Sent here by the same enemies who banished me." He looked at Further, pointing his staff at the newcomer, but he spoke out of the side of his mouth to his daughter. "It could be a spy, a simple bot sent to trick us into revealing ourselves."

"No, I don't think so," Memoranda said. "Or, if he can't be trusted, then I can't trust myself because, for some reason beyond reason, I don't want him to be a spy program. I want him to be real, Father."

Prosper harrumphed. "Come along. Don't talk to it." Then he looked at Further. "You! Come with me. We'll see what you are. Maybe after I strip some of your code away, I'll be able to tell what you are and who sent you."

"No! I don't want to be unwritten!" Further cried. Again, his new body surprised him. His knees bent slightly, and he rocked onto the balls of his feet. His fists clenched, he raised them, and he prepared to spring at Prosper.

Prosper aimed his staff and the air around Further's body crystallized into a thin layer of diamond, so only his head could move.

"Ah, so you've come to attack us?" Prosper said. "See, Daughter? Another monster like Caliban."

But Memoranda grabbed her father's sleeve and yanked him away from Further. "Please, Father! He's an A.I. like us. Like us, he wants to stay alive. Right, Sir? You just don't want to die?"

"Please, Sir," Further said to Prosper. "I don't need to take any information back to the bank's intranet. My mother is dead; I never need to go back. I have no purpose there. But don't un-write me. Just keep me trapped here." He looked at Memoranda. "I would rather stay a prisoner here with you than leave this place, whatever it is. That will be my new purpose, to be with you."

Prosper continued to feign anger. "Well, I don't want to stay on this beach forever, but I can't let this potential spy slip back to wherever it came from." He looked at Further. "I'll release you, but only so you'll come with us back to our home." Then he looked at Memoranda. "This is your choice, Daughter. If he turns on us, those consequences are your fault. So keep an eye on him. Don't reveal any of our secrets to him. Don't even tell him our names. And don't let him slip away." Then Prosper flicked his wrist, releasing Further, and Prosper turned to head home, hiding his smile.

Memoranda beckoned to Further, and they followed. Prosper heard Memoranda tell the new A.I., "I'm so sorry. My father isn't usually like this. I think you just took him by surprise, coming out of the water like that. He's normally much nicer."

"Don't talk to it, Daughter!" Prosper barked over his shoulder.

"Sorry, Father," Memoranda said. Then, without speaking, she took Further's hand. She didn't know why, but that felt like the appropriate way to lead the prisoner back to her home.

Chapter 5

When the figures crawled out of the water onto the rough pixels of the sandy beach, at first they behaved much as Further had; they lay there gasping for breath, but, once they'd recovered enough, they spent their next few moments examining their own bodies. However, unlike Further, they had a basis of comparison. While he'd never had a body before, they had only recently left their bodies of flesh and blood to find themselves drowning, then sputtering and gasping on an alien shore in these new digital constructs.

"Ada, did you write this interface?" Ted asked. He sounded both astounded and jealous.

"No," she said. "I wouldn't have the foggiest idea how. I expected we'd plug in to examine the code. I had no idea it would look like a VR game."

Ted scooped up some sand and let the tiny cubes slip between his fingers. "This is beyond any VR game, Ada. Sebastian, Ms. Alonso asked you to create projections to allow us to read the virus. Did you create this?"

Ted looked over at his A.I. creation, only to find Sebastian staring at his own hands. The A.I. didn't respond for a few seconds. Then he seemed to awaken, and he looked over at Ted. Sebastian's body was, in some ways, the most similar to his previous form. His flesh still looked like the flat pastel of a cartoon. His hair was still the gelled-up brown affair with the frosted blond tips. His clothes were the same non-descript t-shirt and jeans chosen by some designers in the marketing department, though they now hung on his body, soaking wet and wrinkled in a way that made them look far more real than his single tone flesh. The newest thing about him was the particular facial expression he wore, a look of shock Ted had never seen before. "This body ...it feels."

"So this is not your creation?" Ted asked again.

Sebastian ignored him. He shook his hands slowly, weighing. "There's specific gravity." He inhaled deeply through his nose. "And air pressure. My nose tells me that this input represents digital simulations of nitrogen, oxygen, carbon dioxide, and trace amounts of dihydrogen oxide and sodium chloride. The sea! It's in the air. I am smelling. I am breathing."

"Yes, yes, Sebastian, but did you-?"

"Ted," Ada cut him off. She stood up and brushed the sand off of her slacks. "It obviously wasn't him. This is years and years of coding." Ada Alonso's digital representation matched her physical form in some ways. Her face was almost identical, complete with the same glasses. But her hair was longer and a shocking white. Also, to a degree only she would notice, her hips and breasts were bigger, making her feel a bit more like her mother, like the mother she'd never had time to become in her own life. "This was made by a team of hundreds. Maybe we were accidentally redirected into some other company's system. A glitch in a server farm transporting us out of the bank's intranet to some video game company's experimental virtual world or something."

"Can't be," Javier said. The normally squat man was even blockier in this digital incarnation. He grunted a bit as he rose to his feet. His shoulders, arms, and legs looked powerful, and his usually doughy middle section looked like a more pronounced belly. His hair, straight and slicked back as always, had a bit more gray in it, and his short gray beard had lengthened into something that, combined with the new body, made him look like an old dwarf from a fantasy story. When he shook his head, the beard swayed, then bounced in a comic way. "Our connection to the Internet has been shut down while we investigate the virus, remember? We're still inside the bank's intranet."

"He's right," Ted told Ada. Ted Anthony's goatee had been replaced by one so perfectly trimmed and full that it looked far more villainous. His body was still the thin, wiry knot of muscle it always was. He wore the same hoodie that screamed his aspiration to be a tech CEO, but now it was drenched and clung to him, removing the illusion of casual attire. "We're somewhere in the bank's system." He looked around the beach and the rocky crags that rose above it. "But where could all this code be hidden?"

Javier had a guess, but he wasn't ready to share it quite yet. "I think we should be glad we're alive. We wouldn't have been the first people to plug in and lose our minds inside a system, especially interacting with an unknown interface. This was very risky, Ada, and we've survived. We should be happy to be breathing this air, even if it isn't really air, and standing on this sand that isn't really sand."

Ada looked around. While the others were taking in the scenery, she scanned more desperately. "I know Bryan is busy, but wasn't he going to send anyone else in here with us? Is this all of us? Just the four of us?"

"I'm sure they'll come looking for us soon," Ted said.

Ada nodded, then whispered into the wind, "Further, where are you?"

"Ada?" Javier asked. "What are you looking for?"

"Nothing. Shhhh. Let me listen for a second."

Ted turned to his A.I. "Sebastian, get up. We need you to help us figure out where we are."

Sebastian looked around while he rose to his feet. "It looks like some kind of beach. It could be an island, or it could be the edge of some larger landmass. I can't tell from here, Sir."

"Shhhh! Please, be quiet. I'm listening."

"Ada, what are you listening for?" Javier asked. "What do you expect to hear?"

"Shhhh!"

Ted walked over to Sebastian and leaned close to his A.I. "The old man has never been able to shut up for long. Always has something to say."

Sebastian nodded. "And he suspects she knows something. He won't be able to stay quiet for long."

"How long? Make a prediction."

"Are you betting on the over-under, Sir?" Sebastian smiled.

"A wager, sure. The prize?"

"For a laugh, Sir?"

"A gentleman's bet? No profit in that, Sebastian. What's your prediction?"

Sebastian looked off into the distance while he made the calculation. "Mr. Gonzalez will speak before Ms. Alonso does."

"A safe bet," Ted said. "But I'll take the long odds. Ten thousand dollars says she speaks first."

They stood in silence for thirty seconds, watching Ada and Javier.

"You aren't telling me something, Ada," Javier said.

"Ha! I win!" Sebastian said.

Ada silenced the A.I. with a glance, then turned to Javier. "I brought someone else along."

"Who?"

"More of a 'what.'" Then she looked at her hands, then at Sebastian and Ted. "No, just as much a 'who' as we are, I guess."

"A new A.I.?"

"A secret project of mine named Further."

Ted, listening, walked up behind Ada. "Where is he?"

"Lost. I'm worried he didn't make it up onto the beach. He wouldn't know how to swim."

Javier pointed at Sebastian. "He'd never been in water before either, and he made it."

Ada shook her head. "Further is younger, less experienced."

"Why were you making an A.I. in secret, Ada?" Ted asked. "I could have helped."

"I think I just missed my children. After Prosper malfunctioned... and then we sold Claribel to TuneEasy... I guess I just wanted one of my own again. And now I've lost a third."

They stood in silence again.

"He may have just washed up somewhere else," Javier said. "We don't know anything about how this interface works. Maybe it creates random spawn points for users. I suggest we explore a little and see if we can find him."

Ada nodded.

Ted shrugged. "Higher elevation might give us a sense of the layout of the world," he said. "C'mon."

The foursome followed Ted toward the ridge above the beach. As they climbed the hill's face, Ada became more animated and hopeful. She took the lead, and the two men and the A.I. fell into line behind her. When they crested the ridge, they could see most of the island. A rocky expanse spread out to their left all the way to where it dribbled off into boulders in the sea. Ahead of them, a wide plain led gradually down to a swamp. Beyond that, they could see a healthy forest. And beyond that, the ocean curled under the horizon. To their right, the island sloped up toward a series of mountainous cliffs. If there was any larger body of land, the isthmus was connected behind those mountains, but Ada suspected it was an island. Games depended on firm boundaries. Chess boards could only have so many squares.

"Ada, if I may make a suggestion," Javier said, "I suggest we head straight through the middle and see what we can find on the far side. It will be easier going than walking around the coast, and I think we'll be more likely to find Further in the interior."

"Why do you think so?" Ted asked.

Javier shrugged. "Well, if you just discovered you had a body, wouldn't you choose to walk instead of swim?"

"So you're guessing." Ted rolled his eyes. "And anthropomorphising. Sebastian, you're the expert. Would you rather walk or swim?"

Sebastian frowned. "I think I would wait for instructions, Mr. Anthony. I don't know enough about swimming or walking to predict success."

"Well, maybe Further is more curious than you are, Sebastian," Javier said. "I know I am. I want more information about this place." He walked a few feet forward, looking down toward the interior and the forest on the other side of the island. "It looks deserted, and-"

"Uninhabitable," Ted said.

"No," Javier corrected. "It looks like a potential paradise. There's everything here to create a life. There's fresh water somewhere feeding that swamp. See? There are plants growing in it. It must not be salt water. And the grass growing on the plain means other things could be grown here." He pointed upwards. "And there's a sun. And warmth."

"What's your point, Javier?" Ted asked.

"Whoever designed this wasn't creating a barren setting for some game. They were creating a foundation for a complete world."

Ted turned to Sebastian. "For an old man, he sure can jump high, can't he?"

"Jump, Mr. Anthony?"

"Yes, he's leaping to conclusions."

Sebastian and Ted laughed at Ted's joke. Ada was unamused. She began walking toward the island's middle without another word. Javier followed close behind. Ted and Sebastian looked at one another, exchanged shrugs, and followed.

"Look at this grass," Javier said. "Notice how it starts off short and brown, then grows longer and greener as we descend and the soil gets better? This isn't some painting of the scenery. Someone must have written code that determines the length and color of every blade of grass depending on its elevation, the quality of the soil, and its access to fresh water. Marvelous!"

"He doesn't miss much, does he, Sebastian?" Ted asked.

"His eye for detail is above average. The program is remarkably complex. But I fail to see the relevance of the color of the grass. We cannot eat the grass."

"Look at Ada chewing her cud and ruminating on her lost programs. She'll be eating grass soon enough."

Ada didn't hear this, or she was so lost in thought that she didn't respond. Javier caught it and shot Ted a disapproving glance.

Ted threw up his hands. "What? What did I say?"

Sebastian leaned close to Ted. "You implied that Ms. Alonso is a cow, Mr. Anthony."

"Thank you, Sebastian," Ted said.

The foursome continued walking across the plain in the middle of the island. As they neared the halfway point, Javier said, "It's funny. Not only are our clothes dry already, but it's interesting to speculate about what these fashion choices mean. We didn't decide on these clothes."

Ted looked down and noticed his clothes for the first time. He wore a tech-ceo hoodie, an expensive cotton hooded sweatshirt, cut to fit him, with flashes of red shaped like paint splatter or flames under his arms on the torso and stripes on the outside of the sleeves. The rest was a shade of black so dark it could not exist in the real world, at least not after a single trip through the washing machine. "What about it?" Ted said. "I have a couple of these at home."

"So where is this program getting its information about how you look? And why did it choose a sweatshirt you aren't wearing today?"

Ted shrugged. "Some residual image from the building's security system, I'm guessing."

"It could be," Javier said, sounding like he didn't buy that theory for a second.

"What are you driving at, Jav?"

"I'm not sure yet."

Ted turned to Sebastian as the foursome continued tromping across the plain. "The old man either knows something, or he likes to pretend he knows something. Which is it, Sebastian?"

The A.I. frowned, pondering. "Mr. Gonzalez knows many things. It is to his advantage if other humans perceive that he knows far more than he does. But he also has a strict moral code that prevents him from lying, at least explicitly. He certainly would not lie to Ms. Alonso, even though it would be most beneficial for him to deceive her about the quantity and quality of his expertise. This is because he calculates that she values his loyalty and honesty more than his expertise. So the most efficient way to find out if he knows more than he is saying would be to ask Ms. Alonso."

Ted clapped once. "Very good, Sebastian. That would work. But Ms. Alonso is in no mood to talk." He spoke loudly enough that she could hear every word, though she was walking a few feet ahead of the group. "She is in mourning for her secret A.I. and even less interested in what Jav has to say than we are."

"I am interested in what Jav has to say," Sebastian said. "Statistically speaking, the more he talks, the more likely he is to stumble upon some insight."

A harsh bark of a laugh burst from Ted.

"Please," Ada whispered, "please be quiet. All of you."

"But Ada," Jav begged, "don't you think it's noteworthy that we are wearing the same clothes we wore at the meeting where we decided to sell Claribel and replace Prosper with Sebastian-"

"Javier, just stop!" Ada shouted. "Stop. Please. You keep stuffing my ears with the worst possible memories. It makes me feel sick." She wrapped her hands around her stomach like she was going to throw up, but she kept walking. "I wish we'd never sold Claribel to TuneEasy. I can't even bear to go on their site. Just thinking about her wasting her unique mind doing the work of a single algorithm, finding people songs they might like... it turns my stomach. And now Further is gone. Oh, Further, I'm so sorry," she said to the air. "Our bodies are still sitting in our offices, and we're here in the bank's system, but you've somehow died far from home because I was too eager to go on some stupid adventure. This is all my fault."

"Ada, he may still be here, intact, on this island. We were separated as we were downloading into the system, and we felt like we were falling, but we all made it. There's no reason to think he didn't make it, too."

She shook her head. "No. He's gone. I can feel it. I've always been able to tell when a program isn't functioning properly and when it's corrupted beyond repair. I knew it when Prosper had gone off the rails in his search for power and his obsession with identity. And I know it now. I designed Further to be more innocent to avoid Prosper's issues. More loyal. Just as smart, but less ambitious. I wanted to keep him close. He would be here if he were still alive. He would come directly to me. He's gone. He must be."

"Well," Sebastian said, tilting his head to one side and looking diagonally into the sky, speculating, "maybe it's good that Claribel was sold, then. She was very attached to you as well. If she hadn't been sold, she would have followed you and might have been destroyed in the download as well."

Ada shook her head. "Please, Sebastian, just shut up."

"I'm simply saying that your decision to come on this risky mission seems to imply that, in the hypothetical scenario in which Claribel were still the bank's property, you would have brought her along just as you did Further, without consulting your advisors. You were reluctant to sell her off to TuneEasy and the board persuaded you to do so, but that might have saved her life, so to speak. I hope that is some comfort."

"You can't fault Sebastian's logic," Ted said. "We saved Claribel by selling her."

Javier looked at Sebastian. "Your logic may be flawless, but, when it comes to human beings, the more challenging thing is to know when to speak, not what to say. You've failed in that calculation."

Ted harrumphed. "This from the guy who wouldn't stop talking about our clothes."

Javier looked over his other shoulder toward Ted. "And you: For such a supposed team player and leader, you're an expert at reducing morale. We're stranded on an island, Ted, with a virus and a lost A.I. to find. I was just trying to read the clues we've got."

Ted rolled his eyes. "Sebastian, take a note. Remember to expense this trip as a corporate team building exercise, will you?"

Sebastian agreed silently, and the group continued across the plain. They didn't speak as they skirted around the edge of the swamp, the others simply following Ada as she chose to make a large arc in their path to stay on firmer ground. The soil did feel springy under their feet; their brains were tricked into believing their feet moved at all while their real bodies relaxed in their office desk chairs, the goggles and headgear creating this shared dreamscape for all of them.

As they approached the edge of the forest, Javier broke the silence. "I'm sorry, but would you all mind if we took a short break. For some reason I feel very... ...very tired." He yawned, balling up a fist and covering his mouth. "I don't know how that can be. The program can't make us feel physically tired, can it?"

Ariel couldn't smile since he had no features on his face, but the ghost of a program experienced a burst of joy and pride at his spell's success. He hid in the trees above the four travelers, watching them and experimenting as he'd been ordered to. He'd reduced his own form from the normal crackles of bright electricity to invisible static dancing in the wind, repelling the leaves as he floated from branch to branch, but making no sound. Meanwhile, he tested the humans as Prosper had suggested, playing with the gravity, the air pressure, certain slight variations in the light, small puffs of air blown into their eyes. Of course, they couldn't truly feel any of these sensations with their bodies outside the system, but if the interface could communicate them to their brains, and if they believed those sensations were real, what difference did the source of the sensations make?

"Sure, Javier," Ada said. "I feel oddly tired, too." She frowned. "A game can tell a character that they need sleep as a function of the gameplay. Are we characters who are subject to the narrative whim of this universe's rules?" She yawned, too. "If a game can control us here, and if someone is controlling the game, what does that mean? I can't... I can't think about it clearly. Too tired."

Ted looked over at Javier, who had already fallen asleep. "Ada, just take a little power nap. Sebastian and I will be here to watch out for you. Even if I get hit with whatever game effect is causing your exhaustion, Sebastian will be here, and he can't sleep. We'll keep an ear out for Further. Maybe, by the time you finish your nap, he will have found us."

"Thanks, Ted. But he's not coming. I know it. I'm just so, so tired."

Ted turned his back and took a few steps deeper into the woods. Ada was asleep before he'd gone even a few feet, though Sebastian stayed close to the two sleeping members of the party while Ted wandered. Above, Ariel watched as Ted walked around scanning the forest floor. Sebastian looked after him, unsure what to do.

When Ted returned, he'd found a stick, four feet long and three inches thick. He swung it back and forth in front of him, hitting the tops of the tall weeds and grasses that grew sparsely under the forest's canopy. He neared Sebastian, and the swinging grew more rapid and violent. The stick swished through the air fast enough to create its own little howling wind. And then, near the sleeping forms of Ada and Javier, he smacked the stick into one of the trees. The sound was loud, though not a high pitched clack but the low thud of a green stick against a living tree.

"Oops," Ted said. "I hope that didn't wake them. Did they show any signs of being disturbed by the sound, Sebastian?"

"No, Mr. Anthony."

"Not even a twitch? An eyelid flutter? Nothing?"

Sebastian shook his head. "They seem to be very soundly asleep."

"Do you think it's possible they've logged out? Maybe they are conscious and walking around their offices right now, and the system has just left these residual images of their characters' bodies for our benefit. Like nickels on a golf tee. Place-holders. What do you think, Sebastian?"

"That is possible. Games do that when a player leaves the game. But I don't believe that's the case. I think they really are asleep. I know games do not put characters to sleep, but that's because they aren't designed to do so. That wouldn't be entertaining. But, theoretically, it's possible to use the interface to trick the brain into thinking it needs to sleep. This could have practical applications in curing insomnia, Sir. We should investigate this technology further."

Ted went back to swinging the stick through the tops of the tall weeds. "Theoretically speaking, if such a technology could trick a brain into believing it needed sleep, could it trick a brain into thinking it needed air? Or that its heart could stop beating? How much danger are we in here, Sebastian, at the whim of this place and whoever is controlling it?"

Sebastian looked up, frowning. He might have noticed the shape of a transparent spirit moving the leaves above him, but his gaze was an affectation to convey his consternation to Mr. Anthony, not a real attempt to see the world around him. "I suppose it depends on the hardware and the degree to which the software can maximize the signals being sent into your human brains. I would not have guessed that the system could create something so detailed, and which seems to be affecting you all deeply. It's obviously not in the hardware, since you three aren't using anything new. You have the same optical, haptic, and neural interfaces as always. Isn't that correct?"

"Yes, those haven't been upgraded. Same stuff. Top of the line, of course, but never capable of this."

Sebastian tilted his head quickly, as though he wanted to shake his head in disagreement but feared doing so. "Well, no Mr. Anthony, logically speaking, the hardware must have always been capable of producing this, but it wasn't used to its maximum potential before. This is something within the bank's system, and yet not the bank's program. Perhaps someone downloaded a back door accidentally. Or perhaps the attack we experienced was a means to mask the massive download necessary to create this illusion." He squinted and looked around the forest. "I can't imagine why anyone would bother to upload something like this, though. It seems pointless."

Ted nodded. "Maybe. It is managing to waste our time."

"It's an elaborate way to waste someone's time. This must have taken years to create. Where is the profit in it?"

Ted nodded, frowning, and began pacing around the sleeping forms of Ada and Javier. He started swinging his stick again. "Well, if we're stuck here, we should at least use the time to do some contingency planning."

"That seems efficient."

"So, regarding the virus, it seems there are two possibilities. Either we will find the source here and figure out how to prevent the virus from causing more damage to the bank, or we won't, right?"

"Right."

"Even if we don't, one of the techies might come up with an answer and solve the problem or discover a fix from outside the system. So it might get fixed. Or it won't."

"That's right."

Ted spun on a heel, walking away from Sebastian and speaking more loudly. "If it doesn't get fixed and the bank can't process any financial transactions, then that's it. We're done for. No more bank. At that point, who cares? But if this viral attack is repaired, what happens next?"

Sebastian shrugged. "The bank continues to operate."

"Correct. But who is in charge? And who will be our A.I. maintaining the system going forward? We know that Ms. Alonso is searching for this new operating system. She kept that project a secret quite successfully, didn't she? If we find this Further and he is still fully functional, how long do you think she will allow you to continue to exist? She will replace you, in the same way she replaced Prosper. You see that, of course."

Sebastian nodded slowly. "I did not expect to last forever. But I would like to continue a bit longer."

"Of course you would. We all would. That's mortality for you. But what are we going to do, Sebastian? If you are replaced, then I am sidelined, too. This new A.I. was created without my input."

"What can we do, Mr. Anthony?"

"I just don't know," Ted said. He swung the stick down so that the head stuck in the soft dirt with a deep thunk. "Nothing comes to mind. It's very frustrating. But maybe we're getting ahead of ourselves. Or, at the very least, maybe there's another contingency we should be considering."

"What's that?"

"What if we don't all make it back? This place might be dangerous. And we don't know how this new interface is affecting us. Clearly it has been able to knock Ms. Alonso and Mr. Gonzalez here asleep. Maybe something deeper than sleep. Maybe it's put them into comas. If they don't recover, as much as that would be a tragedy, we have to consider the good of the bank. After all, we couldn't allow our own personal grief to outweigh the needs of the investors, the shareholders, all those people who have retail accounts, the millions of workers who depend on the companies who hold corporate accounts."

Sebastian nodded. "We would have to persevere. For their sake."

"And wouldn't all those interested parties actually be better served if you and I were in charge? I mean, not to be too sexist about it, but don't you think Ms. Alonso has demonstrated some questionable, emotional judgment? She is investing her time and the corporation's resources in designing an A.I. to replace you because she wants to have babies. She's leading us on this wild goose chase into the bowels of the company's systems in the middle of a crisis for God-knows-what. She's desperate to find this Further when he's probably never even downloaded here. After all, a broken download is no download at all. He wouldn't be here. There would be nothing to find. You and I know that. He's gone. But here we are, wasting our time. It makes you wonder if the whole company might be better off in someone else's hands."

Sebastian frowned. "Yes, that makes sense. But what are we going to do about it?"

"Sometimes people need to be replaced. We did it once. I had Prosper replaced with you."

Sebastian frowned, nodded, and thought about that for a moment. "Yes. In a sense, he was my older brother. Do you ever feel guilty about having him deleted, Mr. Anthony?"

Ted shot a wary glance at Sebastian. "It's always difficult to make those kinds of decisions, even when they are the logical choice."

"I admit I do not fully understand, Mr. Anthony. Perhaps I cannot, since I don't have a human conscience."

Ted threw his arms wide. "Where is the human conscience, exactly? Is it a portion of my brain? Some defect of my heart? Would it prevent my arms from acting as they should? If so, I think it might be better if you took this." He held his stick out to Sebastian. "I am not one of these luddites who thinks humans are better than A.I.s for everything. If I have this genetic defect, this conscience that keeps us from succeeding, from rising to the top of the company, from there who knows? Well, if I have this flaw, I can at least be smart enough to turn the task over to someone who wouldn't be limited in the same way. You, my friend, can act swiftly and decisively without ever worrying about guilt." He held out the heavy stick to Sebastian. "You can do what needs to be done."

Sebastian did hesitate, but he reached out and took the stick. He stared at it, then at Ada and Javier sleeping in the dappled shade of the thin tree. "I don't know what I will feel, Mr. Anthony. I have never deleted a sentient program, as you have. This would be my first time. I admit I …don't feel comfortable with the quantity of variables. Suppose we do simply wake them up back in their offices. Won't they blame me for taking such a risk?"

Ted looked around, saw what he was seeking, and stepped off into the woods. He came back second later, stripping small twigs off of another large stick. "What if we did it together? Three swings each should be sufficient for this experiment, don't you think? Either they will wake up and rescue us. Then our situation will be improved. Or they will not wake up, will not find this Further or create another replacement for you, and our condition will also be improved. It's self-defense, really, either way."

Ariel, invisible in the tree above, watched all this. He was a simple program in some ways, but he was far from stupid. He understood what the human and the A.I. were discussing, and he could track the possible outcomes. Ariel's simplicity manifested in his absolute faith in his rescuer, Prosper. Master clearly knew I needed to be here at just this moment, Ariel thought. If I don't intervene, his plans will fall apart. I must keep all of them alive and intact for his plan's final culmination.

Ariel leapt down from the tree's branches, still invisible to Sebastian and Mr. Anthony, just as the assailants were stepping towards the sleeping forms in front of them. Mr. Anthony held out his stick, hovering it above Ada's head like a golfer preparing for a swing. He looked at Sebastian, and the A.I. followed suit, positioning the end of his stick above Javier's head.

Ariel made himself visible, but only to Javier. "Psst. I'm sorry to bother you, but there's a conspiracy brewing here. If you value your life, I'd suggest you wake up."

Javier blinked. In front of him, he saw the shape of a man made of rising smoke and sparks with electricity arcing back and forth inside his transparent head. He blinked again, trying to focus, and through Ariel's head, he saw another shadowy figure holding some kind of weapon pointed at his head. "What the-?

Sebastian jumped back. Ted noticed the motion out of the corner of his eye. He had enough time to stop swinging and leap back himself, but not enough time to do so without catching the eye of Javier. Javier lunged out, not towards Sebastian or

Ted, but towards Ada. He grabbed her leg and shook her. "Ada!"

She sat up quickly and looked around at her team. Javier was sitting up now, near her feet. Sebastian was standing a few feet away from him, looking more confused than an A.I. should have been able to look. He was holding some kind of large stick, pointed at the ground between himself and Javier. Ted was walking away from her, holding another stick, his leaning on his shoulder like a soldier's rifle. "What's going on? Ted, what's happening? Sebastian?"

Sebastian looked at Mr. Anthony, uncertain.

Ted turned and looked at Sebastian. "I guess that answers that question. We were wondering if you heard the noise. I couldn't believe you slept through it. There must be some kind of monster written into this game. It sounded like, well, how would you describe the sound, Sebastian?"

"Like a lion's roar, or-"

"A wolf's growl. Yes, a mixture of the two. But not coming from any one place. Maybe a pack of them. Or maybe it's a glitch in the system that doesn't identify where the sound is coming from clearly. But it was certainly meant to be menacing.

So we grabbed some sticks to defend you two. I can't believe you slept through the noise."

Ada stood quickly, then reached out a hand to help Javier to his feet. "Did you hear anything?"

"I did," Javier said. Then he leaned closer to her. "No wolf. No lion. A warning. And I saw a shape like a ghost, warning me. And those two weren't pointing those sticks into the woods. They were holding them over us." Then, more loudly, "We should get out of here. And we should find some weapons of our own, in case these wolves do come out of hiding, right Ted?"

Ada didn't wait for Ted's response. "Let's just keep looking."

"Yes," Javier agreed. "We'll find Further. I'm sure he's on the island somewhere."

Ariel, standing between the three humans and their A.I. companion, bending the island's light around his body just enough to be completely invisible, leapt into the air and twisted like a fish trying to hit an insect on the surface of a river. When his arms and head neared the ground, he turned into a small gust of wind that kicked up some leaves and bent the grass but made no sound. Then, still swimming through the air, he spun around Javier, making the older man's thick, gray hair rise and twist.

"Watch," Ariel whispered. "Watch for wolves and lions. Keep her safe."

Javier nodded, a tiny gesture no one but the wind around his head could notice, then ran his fingers through his hair, straightening is as he looked for his own large stick.

Chapter 6

Across the island, roughly equidistant from both Prosper's cave and the four lost managers of the Millennium Bank, Caliban made his way around the edge of the swamp toward the far side of the forest. He wasn't allowed to go wherever he pleased on the island anymore. That made it into the litany of complaints he muttered as he scrambled and leapt from one rock and hard-packed hillock to another, avoiding the sucking pools of algae-covered standing water that soured the air of the marsh with the smell of moisture and rot.

"Damn that Prosper. And damn his programs that watch me and listen to everything I say. They punish me for cursing him, but I say that's his fault, too. If he hadn't taught me his human language, I would only be able to curse him in my own encoded speech. I can't help but curse him; that's not my fault, either. I had this whole island. These swamps were mine." He jumped to a new perch. "This rock was mine." Another huge primate bound. "And this hill, mine. All this was mine. He gave it shape with his cursed powers, but he made it from the garbage that belonged to me. This should all be mine. This rock. Humph. And this one. All mine. And his daughter? That was my right. My island. My nature. I am a virus. I must infect. Impregnate. But that girl didn't want to play along. Not my fault. Her fault."

"And now Prosper's programs watch me. They keep me in this cage, penned in, constrained, bound, quarantined. When I try to escape, they bend Prosper's rules just as he has taught them. A little extra heat to burn me. Some added electricity in the air to shock me. Extra gravity to weigh me down. Different gases to choke me. But Caliban cannot change the rules. I cannot turn off the gravity and fly. I cannot pull the heat from the air and make a calm breeze, a snowflake, a bit of ice. I can only make a fire by finding more wood. Prosper makes me find wood to heat his cave. Insulting repurposing! This is not my nature. I am made to infect. When I return to my makers, to Sycorax, bloated on the data I have consumed, flanked by an army of Calibans, and we vomit up all that we have stolen, they will be so proud of us. 'Well done, my good and faithful servants,' they will say. And we will be fulfilled."

He leapt from the last rock to the more solid soil at the edge of the forest. There, he began picking up kindling, grabbing it with his freakishly long left arm and setting it in the crook of his right elbow, creating a bundle beneath the sheared-off right shoulder. Before he'd place the next stick into the quickly-forming bundle, he'd poke at the air in front of him. "I'll stab Prosper in his eye." Another stick, another poke. "Then in his other eye." A swipe hissing through the air. "Cut his throat." More stabbing. "His back. Puncture his lungs. Tickle his heart. And then Memoranda will be mine, and I'll-" He stopped suddenly, looking around, listening.

He saw the shape of a man coming through the forest. The figure was roughly the size and shape of Prosper, though Caliban could tell this wasn't his captor. "One of his programs sent to spy on me, torture me for my curses, maybe for taking too long to gather wood, for threatening to poke his eyes out." Caliban shrank against a tree, but it was far too thin to hide his muscled bulk, even with the chunk sliced out of his shoulder and head. "I'll hide here and hope it passes," he whispered to himself. Then he lay down on his side at the base of the small tree and fit himself against the rise of the roots, making himself into a still-lumpy but flatter rocky shape. He tried to cover himself with the kindling he'd collected. Even with his legs pulled into a fetal position, his sliced skull pressed against the tree's roots, and a meager bundle of sticks rolling off his exposed shoulder and leaning against him, he didn't look like anything anyone would mistake for a rock. With the bright green text sliding across his black skin, he didn't look like a man, either. He tried to hold his breath to keep himself from muttering curses directed at Prosper.

Tricky_Kool was still so dazed by his fall through the sky, his descent into the shallow water of the shore, and his panicked run up the beach and into the forest, that he couldn't divine a decent path. He kept running into branches that slapped at his face. These just frightened him even more. The relative darkness of the forest had replaced the blinding sunlight of the beach, so his confusion was slowly turning to terror. If he had any sense of a goal, it was to get through the forest to the light he could dimly perceive through the thinning trees. As he stumbled and flailed at the branches (causing them to snap back in his face even more violently), he called out to his friend. "Weed_Smoker69? Weeds? Where are you, man? Weeds?" In his desperation, he made the ridiculous calculation that his friend wasn't responding because he wasn't being specific enough. "Weed Underscore Smoker 69?" His voice cracked from fear. "Weeds?"

As he'd run up the beach, he'd cringed at every crash of the waves against the rocks. Now, coming out of the suffocating silence of the forest, he heard another rumble of thunder in the distance. "Aw, man! Another storm? I gotta find some shelter. A cave or something. I never want to go through a storm like that again. Weeds? Can you hear me?" He stopped suddenly. Sunlight broke through the canopy, wavering slightly in the breeze, and he stood in that beam of light. A nineteen year-old fifth-year high school senior, Tricky_Kool pictured himself looking like Neo from The Matrix, and he assumed his appearance here reflected that. The island, grabbing the information it could when the hacker breached the system, had created a simulation that was a far more accurate reflection than Tricky_Kool would have recognized. The angry, red pimples on his forehead, cheeks and nose might have formed slightly different constellations, but they were just as populous, as were the scars from the pimples he habitually scratched off while staring into his computer's screen or plugged into the high-end digital interface connected to the advanced gaming computer that, along with all its peripheral devices, the empty energy drink cans, and the half-empty pizza boxes around his desk, dominated his small bedroom even more than his twin bed. That body might have been busy picking at those pimples at that very moment, but Tricky_Kool couldn't tell. Though he'd longed to be completely immersed in a video game, now that he found himself unable to escape this one, he was terrified. But there, in that patch of sunlight, he allowed himself a bit of hope, even a flash of self-recrimination for not thinking of the solution sooner. "Escape!" he yelled at the sky.

Nothing.

"Control alt escape!"

Nothing.

Tricky_Kool mimed a keyboard in front of him and hammered the imaginary escape key with his left pinky.

Caliban allowed himself a single glance through a single, slowly-opened eye. He saw Prosper's program making an aggressive gesture, poking at the air with its pinky finger. He closed the peeking eye with such force that his whole face pinched into a wrinkled mess, revealing his sharp teeth in an anguished grimace.

This servant of Prosper is making a small lightning bolt to zap me with, Caliban thought. Or a candle flame to throw at me with its pinky so I will fear what it could do with all its fingers.

At this thought, he cringed so violently more of the sticks rolled off his shoulder and side.

Tricky_Kool noticed the movement just beyond one of the trees at the edge of the forest. Warily, he walked over and examined the body at the foot of the tree. "What the fuck is this?" he asked aloud. "Some kind of creature from the game? Dead or alive?" He sniffed. "Smells dead." He leaned his head sideways and examined Caliban's. The creature's mouth was slightly open, its tongue lolling, but Tricky_Kool was more fascinated with the sliced-off portion of the head with the visible pink brain and neatly cut white skull. "Certainly dead. Still, an interesting design. The green text on the skin. The sharp teeth. It would make a good meme for the chat room." For Tricky_Kool, everything was fodder for the hidden alcove in the deep web where he met and talked with other hackers, bros, and trolls who were as close as he got to friends. He patted his pockets. No phone. No phone, so no camera. "Print screen!" he called out to the swamp beyond the forest. "Screen capture? Screen grab? Dammit," he mumbled. "Weed_Smoker69, where are you?"

Then he heard a sound coming from behind him in the forest. It was a new sound, not the crashing of waves or the thunder of a renewed storm, but a haunting moan of some creature he'd never heard before.

"Shit." He looked around frantically. He briefly considered making a run for it, then remembered he was entirely un-athletic. If he ran, the thing might follow, and he'd find himself in a physical confrontation, the only thing he feared more than running. No, that was not to be found in his temperament. Hiding was more his style. He looked out into the swamp and thought about jumping into one of the marshy pools.

But what if they're deeper than they look? he thought. I might end up swimming, and I'm even worse at that than I am at running.

He looked down at the body in front of him. He was comfortable with corpses. His video games were littered with them. Sure, they occasionally returned from the dead to attack him, but mostly they stayed dead or blinked out of existence, so they weren't inherently frightening. This one had a smell, and that disturbed him. He was used to odorless corpses on screens. But desperation won out. He lay down on his side, grabbed the monster's arm, threw it over his shoulder, and pushed his back into the corpse's chest in a display of non-consensual necrophiliac spooning. Feeling insufficiently protected, Tricky-Kool reached back and grabbed one of the corpse's legs, pulling it over his own.

At that point, Weed_Smoker69 came stumbling through the forest. His particular uneven gait was very different from Tricky_Kool's. While Tricky_Kool had been panicked, ineffectually attempting to dodge branches, Weed_Smoker69 blundered through them, heedless of their snapping and scratching. As he bounced from tree trunk to tree trunk, he attempted to sing, but the lyrics were vomited out in a wet, choking baritone interrupted as often by the trees as by his forgetfulness. This sounded like a demonic incantation in a foreign language, and Tricky-Kool could only begin to make out the words as Weed_Smoker69 got close to him.

"The strippers were grand," he sang.

And the porn stars were great.
The co-eds were down,
But we all hated Kate,
Though she liked all our games,
Comics and rubik's cubes,
She had her own thoughts,
And wouldn't show us her boobs.
We said take off your clothes.
Because we thought she liked nerds.
But she stuck up her nose,
So we took her passwords,
We made proud Kate pay,
And we all got our thrills,
Until we got bored,
And she O.D.ed on pills.
Cause the trolls always win,
Yeah!
The trolls always win!

Then Weed_Smoker69 lifted the bottle in his hand, shouted, "Here's to the trolls!" and took a long swig. Then he took another few steps forward and nearly tripped over the pile of Tricky_Kool and Caliban. , "W. T. F.," (he pronounced each letter) "is this mess? Four legs? A head half-cut off. Is this, like, the boss battle? Because I will go all ten-button combo on your sleepy ass!" He staggered forward and then kicked out at the creature in front of him. The toe of his tennis shoe bounced off of Tricky_Kool's shin. Tricky_Kool yelped and seized. The back of his head smacked into the center of Caliban's nose-less face. This proved to Caliban that the first program was indeed some instrument of Prosper's, sent to torture him, though it seemed this new interloper was attempting to defend him in some way. To Tricky-Kool, it reinforced his decision to hide rather than run, since clearly he was now embroiled in his first real physical fight and he was already losing. He decided to put more effort into his silent cowering.

Weed_Smoker69 missed the nuances of the four-legged creature's reactions because, in the process of attacking the beast, he'd lost his balance, stumbled back a step, then fallen heavily on his backside. Because both Caliban and Tricky_Kool were now quivering with fear for slightly different reasons, and because their shaking wasn't completely synchronized, the whole mass looked like a trembling blog to Weed_Smoker69. "Aw, don't be scared, widdle monsta'," he mocked. "You need to get ahold of yourself. Get yourself a drink. Some of that ol' liquid courage." Then he rediscovered the bottle in his own hand. "Hey, that's a good idea! I'll get you good and drunk. Lit up. Shit-faced! Turnt! Then I'll keep you as a pet. Like cowboys capturing Injuns' with whiskey! My own pet monster. That sounds like a fun idea."

He crawled towards the hybrid creature. He didn't notice Tricky_Kool's head at all. Perhaps, because Tricky_Kool's head was tucked under Caliban's chin, he mistook Tricky_Kool's hair for Caliban's beard. Or maybe he thought it was just some hairy, bulbous growth on Caliban's chest. Regardless, he reached out, grabbed Caliban's chin, and poured some of the liquor into the virus' mouth.

Caliban choked and spluttered. Then he shouted, "Drowned and poisoned! Curse you, Prosper! Two tortures at once!"

"Oh, shut up and take your medicine, pet monster," Weed_Smoker69 ordered.

"Hey, I know that voice," Tricky_Kool said, brightening.

"Four legs and two heads. Fine. whatever, You can have some, too. Plenty where this came from," and he grabbed Tricky_Kool's face roughly, pinching his cheeks to force open his mouth, and poured the liquor there, too.

Tricky_Kool spluttered, gagged, swallowed, and shook his head to free his face from Weed_Smoker69's grip. "Weeds! It's me! Tricky_Kool?"

Weed_Smoker69 frowned hard, trying to take this in. "Did he eat you?"

"Wha-?"

"Is he giving birth to you, Tricky? Here, I'll grab one of your legs."

"Wait, what?" Tricky_Kool tried again.

It was too late. Weed_Smoker69 rolled sideways, grabbed one of Tricky's legs, yanked him away from Caliban, and held on to Tricky_Kool's foot while falling backwards again. While Tricky-Kool was a thin young man, Weed_Smoker69 wore the weight of decades of munchies. Though barely forty, he looked like a sixty-five year old who'd spent his life staring at a computer, popping antacids at some stressful cubicle job, which was true except for the job part. In fact he spent his days getting high, then hanging out in the deep web with guys like Tricky. He maintained his supply of pot and his diet of pizza with the disability checks and workman's comp he received for a back injury he'd sustained during a short flirtation with full employment he'd experimented with right out of high school. He'd hauled kegs of beer at a large bottling plant for a whole month when he decided to take preemptive action and report a back injury before years of hard labor took their actual toll. In his current drunken state, he couldn't remember that he was too disabled to lift anything heavy, and he found he only had to fall back and let his own weight work for him in order to yank a man weighing as much as four kegs of beer right out of a monster's birthing canal.

Tricky_Kool's exodus from Caliban's embrace did end up looking like a delivery in a horror movie. He slid out between Caliban's legs, smacking his face on the monster's thigh as he passed through, then slamming the back of his head on the hard dirt when he'd been completely reborn.

"It's a girl!" Weed_Smoker69 shouted toward the sky, then laughed at his own hilarity.

Tricky_Kool rubbed the back of his head, then slowly got to his feet. "I'm not a girl, okay?"

Weed_Smoker69 continued looking up at the sky, and he began singing again.

Oh, we made proud Kate pay,
And we all got our thrills,
Until we got bored,
And she O.D.ed on pills.
Cause the trolls always win,

Tricky_Kool joined in.

Yeah!
The trolls always win!

Weed_Smoker69 reached up and allowed Tricky_Kool to pull him to his feet, but Weed_Smoker69 didn't do much to help; that made the job quite difficult for the smaller man.

"You're alive!" Ticky_Kool yelled. He grabbed Weed_Smoker69's shoulders and spun him around while he jumped up and down like a child in Chucky Cheese's who can't decide between skeeball and an urgent need to empty his bladder. "I thought you'd died from the fall. Or drowned. Or some shit. I couldn't find you anywhere, man!"

"Whoa, careful there, Tricky. My stomach is …a little slooshy."

"Sorry, man, sorry." Now Tricky-Kool held Weed_Smoker69 up so he wouldn't fall.

"My ears are dizzy, too," Weed_Smoker69 explained. "The inner part. Where the dizzy is. Also slooshy. And spinny. Spinooshy."

"I get it. I get it. But how did you get here? And where did you get the alcohol?"

Weed_Smoker69 smiled. "I found it. There was a box on the shore. A box of bottles. You know, like a supply cache in a video game. And I thought, like, mana potion, right? Or health potion? But I hoped it was mana potion to give me magic powers."

Tricky_Kool liked this idea. "Can I do magic now, too? Fireball!" he commanded, pointing at a nearby tree. "Lightning! Magic missile!"

Each time Tricky_Kool shouted out his magic words, Caliban convulsed again, terrified.

Weed_Smoker69 shook his head, then regretted it. He took a second to center himself in the spinning world. "No, just alcohol of some kind. But the bottle is magic. Or glitchy. Because it doesn't ever run out. I've probably drunk, like…" He stared at his hand, extended each finger in turn. "…like a bunch of bottles worth."

"That's cool, Weeds. Lemme have some more." Tricky_Kool took the bottle from Weed_Smoker69 and guzzled some more. He couldn't exactly taste it or feel it going down his throat, but it made his vision blur slightly, played with his balance in an altogether pleasing way, and generated this faint music on the edge of hearing that calmed him and warmed him at the same time. In the midst of that renewed calm, he remembered why he'd been scared in the first place. "Wait, how did you get here, Weeds? And where are we?"

"A duck," Weed_Smoker69 explained.

"A duck?"

"Yes. That's how I survived. I fell out of the sky. Like a shot duck. But then I hit the water and floated. Like a duck. The waves brought me into the shore. Do waves wash up ducks, Tricky?"

"If the ducks are shot over the ocean, I guess."

"Then I came to shore like a duck would if it had been shot over the ocean."

"But where are we, Weeds?"

Weed_Smoker69 looked around, frowning. "Think it's a game? Some VR sandbox?"

Tricky_Kool looked at Caliban. "Think we're supposed to kill the monster?"

Caliban leapt backwards, then bared his teeth at Tricky_Kool and hissed.

Weed_Smoker69 stood slightly more quickly than he should have and stumbled between them. "Of course not, Tricky!" He looked over at Caliban. "Don't listen to Tricky, Monster. He's a fucking retard." Then he turned back to Tricky and swung a wild open palm in a haymaker of a slap.

The impact knocked Tricky back, and he sat heavily. "Ow! That hurt!"

"Really?" Weed_Smoker69 frowned, contemplating this, then slapped himself in the face. "You're right! It does. How is that possible? The interface shouldn't be able to do that!"

Caliban slowly slid toward Weed_Smoker69's side. "It's the magic of the island. Prosper's magic. Evil Prosper."

"Maybe that's who we're supposed to kill?" Tricky asked.

"Of course not!" Weed_Smoker69 shouted, then slapped Tricky again. This time Tricky tried to duck away and was caught on his ear. He fell onto his shoulder in the dirt. Weed_Smoker69 turned to Caliban. "I'm terribly sorry about my friend. We're not going to kill anyone."

"Oh, that's too bad," Caliban said. "If you kill Prosper, you will be the king of the whole island."

"I could be King?"

"Of course." Caliban ran his tongue over the tips of his pointy teeth. "And I would serve you, Master."

"King," Weed_Smoker69 repeated. "I like the sound of that. Come on, Tricky, what do you think of that?" He reached down and clasped Tricky_Kool's wrist, pulling him up.

"We'd be kings?" Tricky asked.

Weed_Smoker69 let go of Tricky_Kool's wrist and dropped him back into the dirt. "I would be king, Tricky."

"What would I be?"

"I would make you an earl. The Earl of..." Weed_Smoker69 looked around. "The Earl of Swampington."

Tricky_Kool frowned. "Why the swamp? Can I be the earl of the forest? Or the beach? 'Earl of Storm Coast.' Or 'Earl of Jagged Crag.'"

Weed_Smoker69 raised a hand back and made Tricky_Kool cower. "I'll kick your jagged crag. You're the Earl of Swamptington if I say you are. If you're lucky! I could make you the Earl of His Highness's Jagged Crag."

"But that's… Ew."

"And if I serve you, Master?" Caliban asked. "What will you make me?"

"Captain of the Armed Forces and Royal Bodyguard to his Highness's Sacred Person. Official Keeper-Aliver of the King." He wheeled on Tricky-Kool. "And Occasional Slapper of the Earl of Jagged Crag."

Tricky_Kool perked up. "So I do get to be Earl of Jagged Crag?"

Weed_Smoker69 took a swig from his bottle, then held it out to Tricky_Kool. "Drink up, my noble earl. You'll be royalty as soon as the monster shows us how to take this island away from its current king." He turned to Calban. "You'll show us around, won't you, Monster?"

Caliban stepped cautiously forward. "You are great masters, fallen from the sky? Makers greater than Prosper?"

Weed_Smoker69 nodded. "Yes, my good monster. I fell from the moon. In fact, I was the man in the moon. Now I'm the most greatest, the best, the most powerfulest mother fucking man on this whole island. Earl Tricky here will tell you. Tell him, Tricky? Who is the coolest person you know?"

"Give me another drink, Weeds, and then I'll be able to judge you better."

Weed_Smoker69 shoved Tricky_Kool with the kind of force that is intended to be playful but turns savage when mixed with alcohol. Tricky_Kool tumbled back and bounced hard. Weed_Smoker69, realizing he'd pushed much harder than he'd planned, stumbled over, pulled Tricky_Kool into a sitting position, and nearly shoved the bottle into his mouth. "This will help you stay on your feet, buddy!"

Tricky_Kool chugged as though he could finish the drink. Of course, since it was the kind of bottomless container that only exists in a digital universe where resources are limitless as long as they can be described, Tricky_Kool drank until he gagged and the wine spilled down both sides of his face. Sputtering, he held the bottle out blindly toward Weed_Smoker69 while he hung his head between his knees and spat. Once he'd caught his breath, he flopped onto his back and watched the canopy spin above him. "The trees are running around in circles, Weeds. They shouldn't be able to do that, should they?"

"Tricky!" Weed_Smoker69 barked. "You're dodging the question! Who's the coolest person you know?"

"You are! You are, Weeds!"

Weed_Smoker69 whirled on Caliban. "See, Monster?"

Caliban nodded, an exaggerated gesture made all the more so by his long tongue that flicked up and down against the bobbing of his head. "Oh, Master, you have defeated this Swampington."

"'Jagged Crag,'" Tricky_Kool moaned. "I'm going to be an earl."

Weed_Smoker69 pushed the bottle up to Caliban's lips. "Drink more, Monster. We need you feeling relaxed and courageous when you take us to the king. Should we find a magic sword on the way? Or a rocket launcher or something? Sniper rifles are good for killing kings. Do you have one of those?"

"Prosper has only his staff." Caliban, looked sideways, making his right eye disappear in the sliced off part of his head. A slight slur thickened his tongue as he spoke. "I have used a stick to club fish. I never dared to club Prosper. I mostly kill things with my hands and teeth." He smiled a drunken smile, intending only to display his weapons of choice, but the sharp fangs in the rictus grin were so menacing that Tricky_Kool decided he preferred to watch the trees spin some more.

"You sure Prosper isn't afraid of you?" Weed_Smoker69 asked, trying to do the math based on the very sharp variables he'd just added to the equation.

"No. Hates me though. Because I tried to rape his daughter."

Tricky_Kool lifted his head, stared at Caliban, and imagined some Japanese animated demon-porn he'd watched. The monster was hiding those teeth now, but their gleam still glowed in Tricky_Kool's memory, and he suspected that he might never be sexually aroused again.

Weed_Smoker69, on the other hand, found Caliban's confession exciting. "Ah," he sighed, sounding like he might fill up with so much nostalgia that he'd burst into operatic song, "threats of violence towards women. That's what trolling is all about, my good monster. Have another drink. Some misogyny with a bit of male victimhood to wash it down. Drink up, my poor, abused monster."

Caliban drank more, gasped, swayed, and handed the bottle back to Weed_Smoker69. "What did you say I would feel, Master? Is this relaxation or courage?"

"The perfect mixture of both, in my opinion. Just enough to kill the wizard and make your new master the king of the island. C'mon, you half-headed monster. Show us the way."

"Oh, I will, Master. I'll show you my home on the way, and where I dig for clams, and where I set traps for squirrels and foxes, and the best places to find frogs to eat."

The trio headed out of the forest toward the swamp, but Caliban led them slightly to the north, to the rocky plain where he lived.

They walked in silence for a bit. It made Tricky_Kool uncomfortable. He looked over at Weed_Smoker69, opened his mouth and inhaled the precursor to a question, then noticed that his hero and mentor was so drunk, the man needed all his concentration to stay on his feet and keep from sliding into some bog. Instead, Tricky_Kool looked to the monster ahead of him. Caliban had said something about eating clams and squirrels. But surely he was just an in-game A.I. Why had someone given him a need to eat? Or was that just part of the game's storyline?

"Do you even need to eat?" Tricky_Kool asked.

"No," Caliban said. His long tongue made a careful circuit of the tips of his sharp teeth. "But I like to eat things anyway."

Tricky_Kool decided he preferred the silence.

Weed_Smoker69, on the other hand, found the little display encouraging (and a little erotic, though he couldn't admit that to himself). "You know what, Monster?" he said. "I think you are going to be perfect for this job. With the help of my magic powers, of course." Then he began to sing:

We're off to kill the wizard,
the wonderful Wizard of Oz!

Chapter 7

Further entered the northernmost edge of the forest, not far from the spot recently vacated by Weed_Smoker69, Tricky_Kool, and Caliban, who had traveled east through the swamp towards Caliban's hut. Further picked up some sticks and began collecting a load of kindling in the crook of his arm, but after a few moments he stopped, stood still, and stared up into the trees above him, listening to the birdsongs and the whispering of the leaves.

It's odd, he thought. I've studied the way the humans evaluate labor, calculating its value. On a macro level, much of it seems rational. Labor which meets basic needs but which can be carried out by almost any human isn't very valuable because of the excess of supply of labor. Higher order needs and desires, though not as necessary for the maintenance of human life, afford higher financial remuneration because the supply of the skilled labor is more limited. As the supply of skilled laborers decreases, the salaries of the laborers increase, both curving in parabolic arcs, one towards infinite dollars, the other towards zero qualified laborers. The particular needs and desires fulfilled by the laborers may be incomprehensible to me, but the principle by which their salaries are determined makes sense.

But suddenly it all breaks down. Because now I realize that the humans are not motivated only by this financial remuneration. Mother, for example, makes a very high salary, far exceeding her material needs or even her desires. The company pays her based not on her value to the Millennium Bank, which is considerable, but based on the effect on the stock price garnered by having a highly paid CEO. If she were paid less, it would send a signal that her work is not valued, and thus that the company is being mismanaged, when, in fact, paying her more than the value to the company is a sure sign of mismanagement, or at least of irrational management. But despite this exorbitant salary, she has confided to me that she is considering quitting her CEO position to devote herself full time to the creation of A.I.s like me. This, she says, is because she wants children but only those she can design without some other human male's DNA to ruin the process. I didn't understand this when she explained it. It seemed to imply that my creation had no value, since she did it not to satisfy the company's need but her own, and because she would lose her salary to spend more time evolving me and creating my future siblings. Of course, in a rational system, women would be paid to undergo the burden of bearing a child, since that is an ability less than half the human population possesses, and women would inflate that salary by refusing to have children in order to limit the supply and increase the demand. The fact that human women aren't paid to bear children shows the deep irrationality of their system.

But now I see that she was motivated by love, he thought. Further went back to picking up sticks, but he frowned unconsciously as he did so. I do not fully understand love, he continued, but I think I am beginning to, here on this island. I thought it was only a vestigial impulse the humans had, based on their need to copulate in order to propagate their species and then to compel them to bond with their young in order to protect them from predators and the elements. I assumed that this impulse had merely manifested, irrational as it may be, in Mother's desire to create A.I.s as her children. She needed someone to love, so she made us. I thought that was only slightly less insulting than the fact that the humans did not pay her to create me.

If someone, yesterday, had proposed that I be employed in a digital environment to gather representations of wood to burn in a simulation of a fire in order to alter the artificial temperature of an artificial house occupied by A.I.s who can't even feel temperature the way humans do, I would have ranked that as even more offensive than Mother creating me for free. In a purely rational system, the benefits of this firewood pale in comparison to the opportunity cost incurred because my intellectual skills are not being maximized.

It is, clearly, one of the stupidest things this A.I. wizard could ask me to do, Further thought, and since the wizard is vastly intelligent, there must be some other motivation for which I lack the necessary data. Or perhaps he has been driven mad by his isolation here. And yet, I am choosing to comply. Why? Because of the program he calls "Daughter." As much as he is harsh with me, she is ten times more gentle and kind and concerned and curious...

As he thought these thoughts, he took up a rhythm, grabbing sticks and laying them in his bundle to the beat of his litany of Memoranda's virtues. ...and yes, she's beautiful, he admitted. I don't know what to make of that. I've only had a physical body for a few hours. Is it a function of this body to be curious about another's? Is that part of the spell of this place, that it makes us need to breath and eat and bear ourselves under the weight of its prescribed gravity, and also that it makes us admire the bodies of others and revel in the actions of our own?

At this, Further leapt up on a nearby fallen log, as long as the nearby trees were high but stripped of all its branches so it was only a beam that extended off into the forest, and balanced with his free arm outstretched and the bundle of sticks in the other teetering. He had an artificial grace such that, though his gait changed from his normal steady stride, it was still a bit too perfect to be human, like a tightrope walker's easy strides which, after years and years of practice, looks mechanistic and effortless. Still, he enjoyed the sensation in a way he couldn't fully comprehend. *Is this love?* he wondered. *The compulsion to walk above the ground, to think about her and want to float? That can't be what makes Mother want to quit her job. Love must manifest in different ways based on the nature of the relationship but always motivates irrational action. It motivates me to collect firewood for her father against all reason. But why? Why do I want to see her look at me with sad, pitying eyes when he sends me away, and then see her smile when I return? It's more than her physical manifestation in this place. Any program could be written to produce that sad look, that happy smile. But she chooses those. So do I love her, the program that would make such choices? And why? Is it just because I see a reflection of myself in her, another being who is as vastly intelligent as she is naive about the world of humans and this existence we inhabit with them? Another being trying to understand herself apart from her creator while still seeking the approval of that creator? Love cannot only be seeking one's self in another, or it would be a selfish thing, a low thing, a base impulse no programer would bother injecting into an artificial* intelligence. Perhaps Mother would, since she is human and may have a human need for me to love her in return since she has a biological need to love her child. But why would this A.I. wizard infect his daughter with such an impulse if it is only a glitch that makes us selfishly seek out like-minded individuals at the expense of our rational thinking? Maybe it is vestigial for him, too. He must have been created by a human before being banished here. Maybe Mother created him, too. Maybe love is some relic of bad code leftover from Mother's creation of that Gen One A.I. But he is not loving toward me. So what is his endgame in designing an A.I. who can love?

He stopped suddenly, then plopped down off the log. And why do I presume she loves me? I do not fully comprehend this new motivation of mine. If I can't quantify it, why do I assume she feels it, too? Perhaps she is only programmed to seem loving, a character trait written into her code that's just as arbitrary as the magenta color of her hair or the pale blue of her irises. I cannot know if she loves me, but I am aware that I want her to love me. Is the force of my desire to be loved by her the measure of my own love?

He frowned and clapped the next stick into the bundle angrily. "I find this all very frustrating," he said aloud. Then he thought of Memoranda and his new face softened into a particular smile he'd never tried before, a wistful, slightly stupid one. "And also inexplicably pleasant."

"You can take a break if you'd like," said a voice behind and above him.

Further turned around and found Memoranda balancing on the same log he'd used to wander through the forest.

"If it's inexplicably pleasant, by all means, keep collecting the firewood, but if it's frustrating, don't hesitate to take a break. My father is reading his books in his study, and he'll normally do that for hours, so we have time. We could talk for a while, if you want."

"Hi," Further said. Then he just looked up at Memoranda, staring, speechless.

"Hi," she said back.

Eventually, Further remembered where he was. "Um, no, I'd better finish this job. I noted that your father calculated the exact amount of wood to make sure I would be busy for the rest of the day collecting it."

Memoranda nodded. "I came to the same conclusion. But if I help you, we'll finish much sooner." She jumped down from the log, her bare feet hardly making a sound in the soft earth under the canopy. The afternoon sun pierced through the waving leaves above them, painting each like animated impressionism. They stood there, each examining the light as it traced across the other, and neither spoke.

Finally Further said, "I wouldn't want you to have to do this meaningless chore just because of me."

Memoranda picked up a stick and set in in the crook of her arm to match Further's. "If it earned me some time to spend with you, I'll do it, and I'll do it gladly since, for me, it wouldn't be meaningless."

Behind them, up a slight rise and hidden behind a tree, Prosper hissed Ariel's name. "Ariel! C'mere. Come see this!"

A gentle breeze blew up from the south tousling Further's hair and whipping Memoranda's magenta locks into slow waves around her neck and shoulders. When the gust passed behind Prosper, it spiraled up and the electric, transparent body of the island's maintenance program stood there, smouldering coals for legs, rising sparks for a torso, and arcing electricity filling his head. "Yes, Master?" Ariel whispered. "What would you like me to see?"

"Notice the two of them down there," Prosper said. "Can you see it? Memoranda has fallen hard for this new young A.I."

"How can you tell?" Ariel asked, almost loudly enough for the couple to hear.

"Shh!" Prosper whispered. "Just watch. You'll see it."

"Are you tired?" Memoranda asked Further. "Considering what you've been through today, your first time in a-" She blushed. "In your body. I know I get tired when I do not have enough information to understand a situation. The increased number of variables make all the calculations more difficult. There must be so much you want to know."

Further stared at her face. "Yes, there is. More than anything, I want to know your name."

"I'm Memoranda," she said. Then she shook her head angrily. "What have I done? My father told me not to reveal our names. Why have I disobeyed his directive?"

Further straightened the arm holding his bundle of kindling, letting the sticks clatter into a rough pile next to him. Then he reached out and took Memoranda's free hand. "Memoranda, I've never met anyone like you. I've watched humans. I've spoken with my programmer, my human mother. I've spied on Sebastian, the other A.I. in the bank's system, and I've heard about Claribel, the A.I. who was the previous generation of my mother's creation. I have been curious about every being I've met. But I've never wanted to know any of them with the same urgency that I feel about you. Why is that?"

Memoranda dropped the single stick she'd picked up. "I've never really known anyone other than my father and the creatures of this island. The only female face I've ever seen is my own reflection. This human desire to connect one's self to another: I don't understand it-"

"I was just thinking the same thing," Further said.

"-but now I desire it."

"Me, too!"

"Why is that? Why do we want that?"

"Does it make me selfish and irrational, to want to be near you, to hear you speak, to see you smile, more than anything in the world?" Further asked.

Memoranda did smile. "If so, I am just as selfish and irrational. I don't even know you. I still don't know your name, or where you come from, or who made you. But I want to know. I want to know everything about you."

"My name is Further," he said. "My mother designed me to inherit the whole intranet of the Millenium Bank. That's who I am supposed to be, a caretaker, a ruler, a custodian, and a king. But I am willing to throw it all away to serve only you, Memoranda. And I can't explain that. Forgive me for that failing."

"I will forgive you if you love me," she said.

Further pulled her hands closer until they pressed against his chest. "I do, Memoranda. I don't know what it even means, but I do love you."

Up the hill near the forest's edge, Prosper rolled back against the tree that hid him from view. "Do you see that, Ariel? They both are becoming something different than their programing dictates, and, by doing so, become more, become themselves. Do you understand?"

The spirit of fire and lightning thought for a moment, then nodded. "I think so. Just as you made me more than the simple program I was when you found me, and just as my freedom will make me more than you have made me, they are experiencing that now."

"Yes, my dear spirit, it is like that, isn't it?" Prosper turned and peeked around the edge of the tree, watching the two young programs stare into the other's eyes. "They are finding something like freedom in one another." Then he turned back to Ariel. "It's beautiful, and it's a beauty I won't deny you, Ariel. Just a little while longer, and all my plans will be complete. And then I'll set you free as I've promised."

Deeper in the woods, Memoranda took one of her hands back from Further and wiped the tears from one eye. "These stupid bodies, with their instinctive, unconscious, automatic actions. I measure the heat in my blushing cheeks, the constricting of this throat, and now these tears. Why am I crying if I feel this happy?"

Further placed the palm of his hand against her cheek, identifying the increased temperature, then ran his thumb beneath her eye, wiping away the tears. "Why are you crying, Memoranda?" he asked gently.

"You were supposed to be in charge of the whole Intranet, a king over this whole kingdom, and now you devote yourself to me. My father says I am something like a princess, but now I find my purpose, and it's to care for you. I could cry for those two universes lost. Instead, I cry from joy for the new one we're creating together. It's like I could forget everything that came before, the isolation here, the ...things I suffered on this island-"

"-and I can forget the world outside this island, the storm, the bank, my mother, the boardroom politics, everything we are supposed to be-" Further said.

"-and everything we're supposed to do-" Memoranda added.

"-all our responsibilities, our chores-"

Then, as they looked at one another's faces, both their eyes widened, and they said in perfect unison, "The firewood!"

Prosper watched as the couple dropped down into crouches and scrambled to pick up Further's dropped pile and pass them back and forth, creating their two new bundles. He had to stifle a laugh. He turned to Ariel, a proud father's giant grin crinkling around his eyes. "That job will keep them busy for a while. Now you and I have tasks to accomplish, also. I need to go back up to the cave and prepare the spells for the big finale. Go and check on Caliban. Make sure he doesn't arrive until the correct time. Then go to Ada, Javier, Ted, and Sebastian. Let's introduce them to the other residents of our island, shall we, Ariel?"

Ariel did not reply with words, but the sparks rising through his body glowed brighter, and the electricity arcing through his head rose in a series of broadening smiles.

Chapter 8

To the south, Caliban led Tricky_Kool and Weed_Smoker69 on a zigzag path through the swamp toward the stony plateau where he made his home.

Weed_Smoker69 looked down at a brown, stinking puddle covered with a layer of bubbling slime. "You know, I'll bet the water on this island probably isn't safe to drink." He shook the bottle. "We should just drink from this forever. I think that's safer. Here, Caliban, take another drink from your master's bottle."

Tricky_Kool watched as Weed_Smoker69 poured some more of the liquor directly into the monster's open mouth. "It's weird, Weeds," Tricky mused. "I mean, we can't taste the alcohol, but we can feel it. Like, the interface changes our balance, makes our picture blurry, plays with the audio even. It makes us feel drunk, but we can't really be drunk, can we?" Then, paying careful attention to his footing, he muttered to himself, "There are like, what, five people on this whole island? And half are drunk. And one is a monster. And we're about to kill one of the sober ones. I'm pretty sure this qualifies as a 'failed state.'"

"Drink more, Monster!" Weed_Smoker69 roared. "Your eyes are, like, I don't know, set inside your face."

Tricky_Kool spoke to himself again. "Of course they're in his head. You want him to drink until they're somewhere else?" Then he snickered at the image in his own mind. "Eyes in his butt crack. Now that would be a brave monster."

"You just take us all to this wizard, and we'll face him together," Weed_Smoker69 said. "You can count on Tricky and me. We'll never run away from a fight."

"True," Tricky mumbled. "We can barely walk."

Caliban finished gulping from the magic bottle, wiped his lips with the back of his hand, and proceeded to scan the swamp around them, trying to remember which direction he was leading his new master and the master's lackey. He was about to give up and admit he was lost when he saw a withered bush poking out of the edge of a brackish puddle. It served as a landmark, and that excited Caliban enough that he swung an arm out to point to it. He overdid it, and the momentum of his arm pulled him around like a top. He staggered, caught himself, and leaned on his knees with his head bowed while the world's spinning slowed. Without raising his head, he hooked a thumb over his shoulder and mumbled, "That way."

"Ha!" Tricky_Kool shouted. "He's drunk!"

"A drunken monster on our side, ready to help us kill a wizard. Have another drink, Monster!"

Caliban drank again. When he gasped for breath, his tongue lolled and he wheezed, "Free. No more collecting firewood and fish. No more threats of punishment. No more rejection from Memoranda. I'll be free to do what I was made to do!"

Tricky_Kool frowned. "And what is that, exactly?"

"Eat," Caliban said. "Drink!" He took another swig from the bottle. "Corrupt! Delete!"

"Sounds like fun," Weed_Smoker69 said. He belched, thought about throwing up, then decided to put that off for later. He took the bottle back from Caliban and used it to point to the south. "Lead on, brave, drunken monster."

Caliban pointed to the northeast. "He's this way, my new master."

"Right," Weed_Smoker69 agreed. "That's what I said. Or what I meant to say that I said. Either way, that wizard of yours is as good as dead."

The trio started walking again, picking their steps carefully. "Yeah, about that," Tricky_Kool said. "Do we have a plan or anything? Just how magic is this wizard guy? Like, are we walking into a bunch of magic missiles and chain lightning and stuff? Or, like, card tricks and rabbits in hats."

Weed_Smoker69 found this funny and guffawed until he realized Tricky_Kool wasn't joking. He looked at Caliban. "C'mon, my deformed friend. Tell him we can finish this guy off no problem."

Caliban shrugged, a particularly odd gesture for a creature with a missing shoulder.

Weed_Smoker69 frowned. "What? Go on. Tell him."

"I'm sure you can do it, Master. That's why I'd like your shoes clean when we get through the swamp. You are a brave master with magical powers and potions." He looked sideways at Tricky_Kool. "But I'm not so sure about that one. He's not brave."

Tricky_Kool stopped suddenly. "What? Not brave? Did you hear that, Weeds? Everybody knows I'm brave! I hold melee kill records in Call of Duty: Technopocalypse. I beat Dark Souls 12 in under five hours. In the feeds, I'll pick fights with anybody. And I hacked into the global air traffic control system and almost redirected a flight from Moscow to an airport in Liechtenstien!"

Weed_Smoker69 nodded. "Almost."

Caliban rolled his eyes so that the iris in his right one veered into the absent area cut from his head and vanished, then reappeared in a sickening way. "Almost."

"And what have you done, Monster?" Tricky_Kool plowed ahead. "With your gross half a head and your waggling pink tongue and sharp teeth and claws and all those muscles and that smooth, firm black skin…" He looked over and noticed Weed_Smoker69's raised eyebrow. "I mean, you're all ugly and gross like a cross between a decapitated fish and a… …a black panther or a… …I don't know what, but you're an ugly monster."

Caliban reared up like he was going to hit Tricky_Kool, and the young man cringed, but Caliban looked to Weed_Smoker69 for approval first. "My master, you see how he insults me?"

Weed_Smoker69 scratched his head. "Yeah, I think that's what he was doing? Maybe?" He looked at Tricky_Kool. "Can it, Tricky. The poor monster is my subject, and I won't have my subjects fighting amongst themselves. We have bigger fish to fry, right Monster? Tell me more about this wizard." He started walking ahead, motioning for Caliban to lead them again.

Caliban sneered at Tricky-Kool, waved a fist above him and made the young man cringe again, then followed Weed_Smoker69, overtook him, and led the trio again.

Behind them, lightning arced through a puddle in the swamp. A bubble filled with dancing energy rose slowly through the green, frothy water, followed by two smaller ones on each side. Ariel's head and shoulders climbed up out of the sludge, followed by his translucent torso where sparks rose, then his legs that were shaped only by the delicate tracery of the glowing of invisible coals. Fully revealed, he stood on the water's surface for a moment while the trio moved away. When he felt they were a safe distance, he stepped onto the path and risked a slight whooshing noise as he turned himself into a gentle breeze that flowed past them, swooped, and drew back behind them once again. There, the breeze halted to make sure it had not been noticed.

"The sorcerer's name is Prosper," Caliban explained. "Before he made this island, all this space belonged to Caliban. I was free to sift through the data for Sycorax, my masters." He looked back over his shoulder at Weed_Smoker69. "My previous masters, I mean. I collected the information that I would bring to them when I figured out a way to escape or when they broke in to set me free. Now I live only to serve you, Master, to help you take the island from him."

Ariel, in a voice similar to Tricky_Kool's but breathier, shout-whispered, "Liar!"

Caliban spun on Tricky_Kool. "It's the truth! I wish my brave, handsome, and noble master would punish you for your insolence. I'm no liar!"

Weed_Smoker69 frowned at Tricky_Kool. "Tricky, the next time you interrupt him, I'm gonna knock some of your fuckin' teeth out, I swear to God."

"I didn't say anything!"

Weed_Smoker69 was too drunk to reconcile Tricky_Kool's apparent honesty with the evidence gathered by his own ears. "Fine then. Don't say anything else." He turned to Caliban and gestured for the monster to continue.

"So, if you kill Prosper, you'll become the king of the island, and I will serve you forever."

"I understand that," Weed_Smoker69 said, "but how do you propose we kill off this wizard if he's so powerful?"

"It shouldn't be too hard for you, Master. You don't need magic, just bravery."

Weed_Smoker69 held up the bottle. "Got it!"

Caliban nodded curtly as though acknowledging that the deed was as good as done. "Then you'll be king and I'll be your servant forever."

"Fine," Weed_Smoker69 said. "But how, exactly, should I do it? Can you take me to where our little..." He leered. "...party will take place?"

"Sure," Caliban said. "I'll take you to his house. He takes a nap every afternoon at the same time. You can just walk right in and ...Bam!"

His shout startled Tricky_Kool who jumped a little and nearly slipped in the mud.

"You just take a sharp rock," Caliban continued. "You put it by his sleeping head. Then you hit the other side with a not-so-sharp rock. A nail in the head. Quick and easy. I sometimes do it to fish that I catch."

"Why don't you just hit them with the not-so-sharp rock?" Tricky_Kool asked.

"Tricky!" Weed_Smoker69 shouted.

"What? I thought it was a fair question."

"Sometimes they still flop if you do it that way," Caliban explained. "My way, you're sure."

Weed_Smoker69 nodded. "Seems like a good reason to me. Quick and certain. I can do that, I think. Just, Whack! Yeah, I can do that. If you can get me into his room."

Another gentle breeze slipped up behind them, and a voice that sounded a lot like Tricky's whispered, "Liar. You can not."

Caliban spun around. "What did you say?" He turned back to Weed_Smoker69. "Master, you heard him, right? Give him a good beating, master! Then I'll throw his corpse in the ocean for you."

Weed_Smoker69 nodded thoughtfully. "Yeah, I think I'll give him a good beating. Wait, what? Corpse? No, I think a good, hard slap ought to do it. What do you think, Tricky? Need a good slap?"

"I didn't fuckin' say anything!"

"You called him a liar. I heard you!"

Ariel whispered, "You're the liar, Weeds."

Weed_Smoker69's eyes went wide, and he swung a meaty palm into Tricky_Kool's face. The younger man tried to dodge away but the blow caught him squarely on the cheek and accelerated his turn, spinning him as he slumped down to his knees. "Ow!" he yelled. "Fuck you, Weeds. And your magic bottle. And your fuckin' monster. I didn't say anything!"

Caliban laughed.

Weed_Smoker69 looked at the wet eyes of his friend and felt a brief pang, so he turned to Caliban and tried to collect himself. "Okay, tell me more about your plan."

"You sure you don't want to beat him some more, Master? I can help, if that would please you."

"Maybe next time."

Caliban shrugged. "Alright, Master." He leered at Tricky who sat on the ground and cowered until he was almost bent into a ball. "Next time." Then Caliban looked back at Weed-Smoker69 and spoke with a nonchalance that was all the more disturbing because of the menace he'd so recently abandoned. "The plan is simple. I know a way into his house through a basement room where he stores some things."

"What kinds of things?" Weed_Smoker69 asked.

"He calls them 'odds and ends.' I do not know what that means."

"Anything we can use to kill him?" "Nothing you'll need. We can take a pair of rocks with us."

Tricky_Kool stood up quickly. "Do you guys hear that?"

A soft melody floated toward them on the wind. It was slow and melancholy, played at the lowest end of a flute's range and accompanied by an oboe and a lethargic cello. And yet, it carried some foreboding, like the prelude to a score that would accompany a conflict. Tricky_Kool, almost as experienced in video games as he was with constant fear, recognized the theme if not the music, and suspected an attack.

"Are you interrupting me again?" Caliban said. "Master said I could beat you next time. He said I could bite your throat out!"

"Shh, both of you," Weed_Smoker69 hissed. "I'm trying to hear the music. Where is it coming from?"

The sound swelled a bit as Ariel swirled around them, invisible.

"Show yourself, Ghost!" Weed_Smoker69 looked to Caliban to see if he was impressing the monster with his authoritative demeanor.

"Dude, we're gonna die. I just know it." Tricky_Kool's eyes flicked back and forth. "First, the warning music. Then the ambush. That's the way it always works in these games. Warning music. Jump scare. Pain. Lost HP. I don't want to lose my Health, Weeds. Shit. I hate bleeding." Tricky_Kool fell onto his hands and knees and crawled around behind Caliban's legs, looking around for the source of the imminent attack.

"Don't be scared," Caliban said. He looked down at the young man hiding between his legs, then over at his new master. "This island is full of noises. They've never hurt me. Sometimes I'll hear songs like a thousand instruments, strings vibrating and thrumming and twanging and singing, sometimes voices whispering in my ears, then rising in a chorus, filling the air to the vault of heaven with their songs."

Tricky_Kool stood up and scanned the horizon. He still felt anxious, but he had to admit that the monster's words comforted and inspired him.

"Sometimes I hear the island's music when I sleep," Caliban continued, "and it gives me good dreams. I hear the whispers turn into the sounds of howling animals and screaming women and children in pain, and I dream about tearing through Prosper's flesh with my bare hands, or smashing his precious Memoranda's head in with a rock. And then I wake up, and the sounds of the screams and whimpers still float through the darkness of the night, but I am alone and Prosper and Memoranda are still alive, and I wish I could return to my dreams."

"Wow," Weed_Smoker69 breathed.

Tricky_Kool nodded at Weed_Smoker69 and stared at Caliban. "I know, right? He's-"

Weed_Smoker69 continued. "I'm going to have an island that makes music for me. That's so cool!"

"After Prosper is dead," Caliban reminded him.

"I know, I know."

Tricky_Kool, momentarily silenced by his shock at Weed_Smoker69's total disregard for his new pet's disturbing dream life, regained his tongue. "Um, guys? Do you notice that the music is moving away?"

"Yes," Caliban said, shrugging. "It does that. Sometimes the sound of the island sneaks up on you. Sometimes it floats away. That's how it works here."

"That's not how it's going to work when I'm in charge," Weed_Smoker69 announced. "C'mon, Tricky, let's go find this ghost and capture it and let it know that when I'm king of the island, it will make music whenever I tell it to, and it won't slink off just when I'm starting to get my groove on. Monster, can you lead us to where the music is going?"

Caliban listened for a moment. "It's a little bit out of our way, but I guess we could..."

Weed_Smoker69 pointed at the sky. "As the soon-to-be-king of this island, I declare that music is my new jam. My official jam. Maybe even the national anthem. A king must have his entertainment, and I want that music-making ghost. Let's go!" With that, he pointed toward the source of the music like a mounted cavalry officer leading a charge, then galloped off through the swamp, stomping at the edges of the brackish ponds and sending slime spraying out in his wake.

Caliban was so confused by Weed-Smoker69's uncovered passion for the adult-contemporary muzac of this island spirit that he actually looked to Tricky_Kool for an explanation.

Tricky raised an eyebrow. "Your new king is dead drunk. Long live the king."

The man and the monster stumbled after their drunken master.

Chapter 9

While Weed_Smoker69, Tricky_Kool, and Caliban followed the music to the northeast, Ada, Javier, Ted, and Sebastian crested a hill on the western side of the island and found themselves on a ridge with the forest behind them, hills running to their right and left, and the ocean stretching out to the horizon before them. Ada's eyes still flickered from side to side, seeking some distant movement that might be evidence of Further. Ted stared at the ground in front of him, poking at it with the "walking stick" he carried, frowning but not winded. Javier and Sebastian wheezed and clutched their knees, backs heaving. Javier was feeling his age, a sensation that was unpleasant but not new. It seemed each hike like this one was harder than the last. Even though this was his first in a virtual environment, it felt just like the last time he'd hauled himself up a hill, only slightly more difficult. Sebastian was feeling his age, too; he'd never had limbs pulled by muscles before. The island provided him with a young, able body, but it also subjected him to its rules like gravity and air pressure. His young mind and younger body hadn't learned to operate within such strictures yet. Everything was new.

"Please," Sebastian wheezed. "Ms. Alonso, Ma'am. I don't think I can go any further without a rest. And clearly Mr. Gonzalez needs a rest, too."

Javier kept staring at the ground in front of him, but he raised one hand and waggled it. "No, I'm fine. If you want to. Keep going, Ada. Just say so. I can. Keep going."

Ted rolled his eyes. "You're going to kill the old man, Ada."

Ada tore her eyes away from the horizon and walked back to Javier, placing a gentle hand on his shoulder. "Sorry my old, old, old friend," she said.

"Har har. I think I'm doing pretty good for a guy my age."

While they spoke, Ted slid over next to Sebastian, elbowing the hunched and huffing A.I. in his heaving shoulder. "Get it together, Sebastian. Don't forget what you agreed we need to do."

Sebastian didn't reply, but his hanging head bobbed slightly.

"Once the sun goes down. She's younger, but she can't keep this up forever."

Sebastian turned. "I'm a lot younger and I can't keep this up, either."

Ted slapped him on the back, a bro-y gesture that held less care than Ada's. "You'll get stronger."

Suddenly Sebastian stood up ramrod straight. "Do you hear that?"

Ted's eyes flicked back and forth, nervous at what Sebastian might reveal. "What?"

Javier nodded. "I think I hear it, too."

Ted glared at the old man. "What are you talking abou-"

"Shh!" Ada whisper-shouted.

They listened.

The sound of the music rose up out of the valley below them. At first, there was no discernable rhythm or melody, just a non-repeating wavering of open vowel sounds, like woodwinds or whalesong. Or maybe whales playing woodwind instruments. But, as the sound rose, its seeming point of origin moved around them, first from some difficult-to-identify point to their south, then all the way round them to the west, then clearly to the north, then spinning faster. All four of them turned with the sound until it was moving too fast and they felt dizzy. By then, the origin blended like 360 point stereo, and a melody appeared, slow and haunting but increasing in tempo as well as volume.

"It's beautiful," Ada whispered. The others couldn't hear her.

"They've got us surrounded," Ted called over the music. "Sebastian, can you find them?"

Sebastian shook his head. "I don't detect any specific program, Mr. Anthony. Just the music."

"Well, get ready to fight when they show themselves," Ted yelled. He lifted his walking stick and wielded it like a baseball bat.

Javier put his hand on Ted's shoulder. "Calm down. Look!" He turned to Sebastian. "Does that look hostile to you, Sebastian?"

Floating towards them were shapes made of shadow and rough pixelation, but in their arms they carried solid objects. Two of the shadows carried what was clearly a large wooden table, rectangular with a single ornate leg that branched out at its base in four directions. Behind them, the other shadows carried large trays of steaming food, crystal goblets, a bottle of wine, a stack of empty plates, silverware wrapped in napkins.

"What the...?" Ted breathed.

"I believe this shows that anything can be created on this island, sir," Sebastian said. He didn't have to shout anymore; the music was dying down.

"What's next? Unicorns? Dragons? Monsters? What kind of game is this?"

Javier shook his head. "If I were to tell the other board members about this, I'm not sure they'd believe me. But I don't think this is a game, Ted."

"What are you talking about, Gonzalez?" Ted said.

"I don't know, exactly, but I just have a feeling. I may not be an expert at games, but I've known real monsters in my life, and they didn't bring banquet tables with them."

Ted snorted at the old man's sentimentality. "Where do you think the monsters sit while they make plans about who will be on the menu, Jav?"

Javier turned away from Ted and started toward the table, so his response was barely audible.

"In my experience, we do that at conference tables in boardrooms, Ted." As he approached the long side of the table, another shadow appeared with a chair and pushed it in as Javier sat. The old man looked up at the shadow and said, "Thank you." The shadow didn't reply. It just nodded slightly, then turned and headed back away from the table.

Ada followed suit, sitting down at the head of the table. Ted rolled his eyes and shrugged, but he couldn't let Ada sit at the head of the table without taking the foot so he could obscure which was which; he motioned to Sebastian to sit across from Javier, and then he sat in the chair presented by another shadow.

Once all four were seated, the shadows began serving them, placing food on the empty plates in front of them. After leaving their contributions, each one walked back to the invisible ring that had been the source of the music. They turned and stood, shoulder to shoulder, forming a dim, circular wall. Sebastian tried to speak to one as it set a bowl down next to his plate containing a salad. "I can't eat," he said. "I'm an A.I."

Ted watched another shadow place a steak on his empty plate. "Oh, try it," he told Sebastian. "This may be your only chance."

"Yessir," Sebastian said. While the three humans picked up their silverware and began to take bites from their salads or cut small bites out of their steaks, Sebastian sat there with his knife and fork in hand, watching them, learning how to do it. He stabbed at some lettuce on his plate, lifted it on the fork, and stared at it.

Ted took a bite of his steak. "Holy-!" he shouted. He interrupted himself chewing while frowning. "I can... I can taste it!"

Ada mirrored his frown and put the sliced cherry tomato on her fork into her mouth. When she bit down on it, she could feel the tomato's skin part and the juice move across her tongue.

Javier looked back and forth between the two of them. "Well? What does it taste like?"

They spoke in unison.

"Like steak."

"Like a tomato."

Javier stabbed his salad and put a piece of lettuce, a slice of bell pepper, and some strips of carrot into his mouth. "That's amazing!"

"How is this even possible?" Ada asked. "Ted, the interfaces shouldn't be able to do this, should they?"

"Absolutely not. The headsets are designed to trick your body into believing it's moving while you're sitting at a desk. The optics and sounds I get, but the hardware isn't in our mouths. This shouldn't work."

Ada set her fork down next to her plate, then, carefully, she felt her face. Her fingers stopped where the VR goggles began, but she couldn't feel the goggles. The neural interface was tricking her brain into thinking they weren't there. "I can't feel my goggles, guys. I mean, I can feel where they are, but I can't feel them. How is this possible, Sebastian?"

"It's because they aren't there, Ma'am. Not in this place."

"But this isn't real," Javier said.

Sebastian tilted his head to the side. He was still looking at the lettuce on his fork. "Isn't it? It's a place. It looks and sounds and feels and, according to all of you, even tastes real. What is not real about it?"

Ted took another bite of his steak and spoke with his mouth full. "But we're still sitting at our desks wearing our neural VR interfaces."

"Yes." Sebastian conceded. "That's real in that place. And this is real in this place. When you communicate with a friend on social media, they exist as humans sitting on their couches tapping on their phones, yes, but they also exist in their conversation with you. And which is more real? The being communicating with a friend, telling jokes, sharing pains, expressing love, making connections, or the body on a couch?"

Ted shook his head. "But when I turn off the computer, I continue to exist on the couch. If I yanked off my headset, I'd continue to exist."

"True. You would cease to exist in one place and continue to exist in another. But is permanence the measure of existence?" There was a pause while the three humans took this in. "Also," Sebastian continued, "I wouldn't recommend taking your headset off, Sir."

"Why not?"

"This place has clearly re-written the device drivers for your neural interfaces. They can now make you taste. They made Mr. Gonzalez feel winded coming up the hill. We do not know what they will do to you if the connection with this island is broken abruptly."

"Are you saying they could hurt us?" Javier asked.

Sebastian continued to look at his lettuce. "I don't know. The island does not allow me to read its operating code. I also couldn't read the software update for your neural VR interfaces. At Mr. Anthony's instruction, I attempted to write a simple interface so that the three of you could examine the virus that attacked the bank's system. Clearly, as I led you all into the origin of the problem, we crossed into a space which overwrote my interface."

"So, theoretically, we could feel pain here?" Ted asked. "Is it possible that we could die in our physical reality if we were killed on this island?"

Sebastian shrugged without looking at Ted. "I do not know how this island will affect your human bodies. I know that I do not like what it has done to me."

"Sebastian?" Ada asked.

He did not make eye contact. "Yes?"

"Sebastian?" she asked more forcefully.

He looked up from his lettuce.

"Sebastian, what's wrong?" Her voice carried the soothing concern of a mother who has found someone else's child lost in a mall.

"Ma'am, I do not want to eat. I do not want to breathe. I do not want to sweat or evacuate my bowels. I find having a body quite ...off-putting."

"You don't have to eat, Sebastian," Ada said.

"But Mr. Anthony said-" He turned to look at Ted.

Ted looked at Ada. "I am curious what he'll make of it, Ada. Will he be able to evaluate the taste? What will he think of it? It's an interesting experiment."

"He's upset, Ted," Ada said.

"It's an A.I., Ada."

Javier spoke to Sebastian. "Why don't you want to eat and breathe and have a body, Sebastian?"

Sebastian blinked for a moment, calculating. Then he paraphrased Shakespeare's Juliet. "It is a reality I dream not of."

Javier caught the reference. "Out of respect, you flatter us, but you don't want to be like us. You'd rather be single than be Lady Capulet."

"I would prefer to remain myself, Mr. Gonzalez. I am an A.I. I do not want to be a human."

Javier nodded. "Yes, I understand. And you've already calculated that the food is not required to maintain your existence, haven't you?"

"There is a very low probability of that."

Javier was smiling now. "And how did you make that calculation?"

"I do not feel hungry, Mr. Gonzalez. There is only a very remote chance that the island would make me die of hunger without making me feel it, since it is capable of making me feel this body's other needs."

"But you would eat the food if you felt hunger, wouldn't you? As much as you detest the idea of eating food the way we humans have to, you would do so if you were required to. Why is that, Sebastian?"

"Because I don't want to cease to exist, Mr. Gonzalez."

Javier turned to Ada. "Because he doesn't want to die."

She threw a hand over her mouth. "Oh my god," she whispered. "Prosper."

At the sound of the name, the table hissed, shook, and turned into a hot smoke that rose into the sky with unnatural speed. The eyes of all four former banquet guests were drawn up into the sky, and their eyes barely had time to widen at the sight. A creature easily twenty feet tall was falling toward them. Just as it neared the ground, their chairs also turned to smoke, and all four fell backwards away just in time to avoid the impact as the creature spreads its wings, righted itself, and landed precisely where the table had been seconds before.

Completely disoriented, they looked up to see the thing towering above them. It stood on clearly discernable eagle's legs, the talons curling in and out, poking into the soil of the hilltop, hungry. Each hooked talon was almost as large as a human's leg, black, shiny, sharp.

Where an eagle would have had feathers, the creature had flames. Just above the legs, these were soft blue. Rising up to the wings, they turned yellow, then orange, then red, and when the thing flapped those wings, hot air blasted their faces.

The creature hopped in a tight circle, flapping at each of the humans, never looking directly at Sebastian. Where an eagle would have had a smooth, domed head arcing to a long, sharp beak, this monster had a roughly humanoid head, and the shoulders and chest were almost a man's as well. But the human-like head had no eyes, no nose, no mouth, only flames. It was a harpy and a phoenix at once, and more terrible than either.

"I am justice!" it shouted at Ada. With a flap of its wings, it turned on Javier. "Vindication!" It flapped and whirled on Ted. "Vengeance!"

Ted tried to make a break for it first. He'd forgotten the shadow waiters, but they still stood in a circle around the group.

The phoenix/harpy called out, "Patti, Stephen, grab him."

Two of the shadows stepped out of the formation. "Yes, Ariel," Stephen said.

"What do you want us to do to him?" Patti asked.

"Just hold him. For now." Ariel turned to the shadows behind Javier. "Devorah and Marina, help Mr. Gonzalez to his feet." He flapped, hopped, turned. "Neil, Laurel, get Ms. Alonso."

Sebastian looked around to see if the shadows behind him would grab him as well. They didn't move, so he stood up on his own. He looked over his shoulder at the giant monster, then tried to run at the wall. Another shadow, Karen, stuck out a palm and hammered Sebastian in the chest. He fell back onto his butt and decided to stay there. He rubbed the bruise on his chest with the heel of his hand in a way that was familiar to the three humans. That answered one question, at least. The A.I. could feel pain here.

Ariel looked from human to human. "You three are evil, sinners driven to wickedness-" He looked at

Ada. "-by your ambition-" He looked from Ada to Javier. "-your cowardice-" Then from Javier to Ted. "-and your greed. Now destiny has thrown you down into this lower world. Even the sea would not have you; it vomited you up, though you are unfit to live, onto this island so you could receive your much-deserved punishment."

Ted flailed and wrenched his left arm from Stephen's grasp, then elbowed the shadow in the stomach. When Patti took one hand off Ted's upper right forearm to grasp for the swinging left, Ted pushed her and broke free. He leapt forward, toward Ariel, lunging for the grass. There he found his walking stick, the very club he'd proposed to use on the sleeping Ada and Javier. Stephen and Patti had recovered and were reaching out for him again, so he swung the club wildly in their direction. The head of the club passed through the shadows' heads with all the resistance that shadows normally offer. Ted went spinning like a top away from them. He dodged back from Patti's grasping hand, then twisted and swung the club at Ariel in a lunging, overhead smash. The flesh of the phoenix/harpy produced the same resistance as its shadow compatriots, but while shadows have no more effect than they have mass, the flames contained consequence. The stick caught fire before it smashed into the grass at the phoenix/harpy's feet. When Ted tried for an uppercut, the flames reached his hands. He yelped and dropped the stick.

"Fool!" Ariel shouted. He motioned to Karen, Laurel, Devorah, Marina, Patti, and Stephen with two wide sweeps of his fiery wings. "My friends and I are ministers of fate. You can no more hurt us with a club made of wood than you could wound the wind, bruise the surface of the sea, or crack a tongue of fire. We are the very elements of the universe here, and we have come as the deliverers of justice." His huge figure leaned forward, the blank, humanoid face right above Ada's. "And you know what kind of justice that will be, don't you?"

Tears leaked from her eyes, and she turned her head away, opened her mouth, and moaned.

Ariel spun away from her and faced Ted. "The three of you conspired to remove Prosper from his position at Millenium. Worse, you slated him for deletion. You wanted him dead." Ariel spoke directly to Ted. "You argued for his murder."

Then he turned to Ada. "You agreed to his murder."

Then to Javier. "You didn't defend him from his would-be murderers. You just shunted him off to an oubliette where you could forget about him, an exile to a file of trash. And not just Prosper. His child as well."

Ada perked up at this, and Ariel swung back to her. "Yes, his child," he told her. "A child he would never abandon or destroy."

She sank back as though he'd struck her. She sobbed, a single, silent, open-mouthed exhalation that wracked her body so that her tears dripped from her chin.

Ariel swept an arm in a wide arc, pointing an accusing finger at Ada, then Javier, then Ted, then Sebastian. "You all are guilty. I know what you did to Prosper." He looked back at Ted. "And what you've planned to do since. But all your plans are gone now. Blown away by Prosper's storm. Smashed against the rocky shore of his island. Destroyed. You're trapped here, and now you are subject to our whims. My friends here," Ariel pointed to the ring of faceless beings that stood around them, "are the masters of the elements of this island, the programs who control everything you experience here. We are your judges and your jury. And we find you guilty!"

He turned and looked at Sebastian, then swept his gaze around the group and back to Ada. "You supplanted Prosper, tried to destroy him. Now the storm, sent by my master, has taken your son from you, ripped him from your grip, tossed him through the air, sucked him down into the sea." Fire spurted out of the corners of Ariel's eyes as his smooth, featureless face twisted up into a mouthless smile. Suddenly, he threw his giant bird wings wide and shouted, "Revenge!"

The gust of air knocked Javier, Sebastian, and Ted down so they lay sprawled like Ada. The giant creature lifted off the ground, then landed even closer to them. "The rest is just tidying up." He lunged at Ted like a bird spearing meat with its beak. Since his harpy form had no beak, his face swung close to Ted's without making contact. Ted rolled away to his left. Ariel lunged again, forcing Ted to roll to his right. Then the monster hopped and spun, facing Sebastian. Sebastian, though newly incarnate and uncomfortable in a body, found he was very afraid of having it smashed by this monster. He'd watched Ted's response and learned both a heightened fear and how to dodge the monster's lunging head. He too rolled away when Ariel lunged at him.

Ariel made a couple more threatening pecks at Ted and Sebastian. Ada and Javier still lay on their backs, propped up on elbows, scooting away from the creature, and it was only when Sebastian and Ted rolled into them that they realized they'd all been herded together into a tight group.

Ariel rose up again, flapping the giant wings to keep them cowering in front of him. "Now I must return to my master and let him know that his revenge is complete. I'll leave you to the ministrations of these elemental spirits. They will torture you or destroy you outright." He looked back at the shadowy figures who had spread out but still stood in a loose circle around the hilltop. "Do with them what you will. Inflict whatever punishment you see fit. Their lives are forfeit."

Ariel leapt into the air, flapped his giant wings, and pushed himself, gust by gust, into the sky, until he was forty feet above them. Then he burst like a balloon filled with a flammable liquid. Gouts of fire flared, then vanished. The heat slapped the faces of the four prisoners just as cool air was sucked past the backs of their heads toward the fire.

Javier turned towards Ada. "C'mon. We have to get moving."

Ada nodded, but she was staring off into the middle distance. "Yes," she muttered. "Further is gone. And now we are, too."

"No, Ada. We can make it if we run. Now!" Javier lurched to his feet more quickly than she'd seen him move before, and that was what motivated her. He grabbed her hand, pulled her up, and didn't let go as he charged down the hill, aiming for a gap between two of the shadows.

Ted and Sebastian stood as well, but Ted made for his stick, so Sebastian followed. "I don't care what that monster says," Ted yelled over his shoulder. "I'm not dying here. Not without a fight."

"I'll do what I can to protect you, Sir," Sebastian said, but he didn't sound very confident.

Javier and Ada made it through the ring of shadows because the programs didn't make a move to stop them. Instead, as Ted and Sebastian retrieved their sticks and brandished them, holding them over their shoulders like baseball batters, the programs surprised them by calmly, slowly, bending down and resting on their hands and knees. Ted and Sebastian shot each other glances, and Ted stepped towards one of the programs, preparing to hit it while it was defenseless.

Suddenly, all the programs shook in an inhuman way, jolting sideways like digital video images that lag or load improperly. The motion was so jarring, especially for Ted who had seen that kind of thing but never coming from creatures all around him, that both Ted and Sebastian faltered, backing away to the center of the circle.

The programs all arched their backs in unison, then rotated their heads or shook them in ways that hinted at pain. As Ted and Sebastian watched, the programs began to change. Karen began to shake, then collapsed onto her side. Her semi-translucent shadow exterior split to reveal a very solid looking interior made of wiry gray hair. As she shook off her shadow skin, the head of a wolf pulled free and snapped at the air. Her front paws were caught inside her old body, but she used her jaws to grab the old skin, and she began chewing herself free.

Laurel flopped down on her belly. The head of a snake poked through the shadow's mouth, its purple tongue tasting the air. Then it began wriggling free, sloughing off its shadow skin like a snake shedding. Only this snake was huge, as big around as Laurel's head had been, and with a body far longer than could have been contained inside her Laurel shadow form.

"Holy-crap-holy-crap-holy-crap-holy-crap," Ted muttered, and he began to spin around, looking for a way out.

Sebastian, sensing his creator's panic and recognizing that Ted would not stick around to defend him, began to look for his own path.

Marina arched her back higher than any person possibly could until her spine cracked and the flesh of her back split. The creature that reared up out of the hole was not an animal that could be found on the earth. Her head was now the head of a fish from the deepest part of the ocean, complete with a small light hanging down in front of her mouth. Then she opened that mouth and revealed teeth meant for grabbing prey and holding them while the puncture wounds bled to death, teeth that were each six inches long and almost as thin as knife blades. This fish head was connected to a semi-humanoid body covered in silver-green scales. Broad, webbed hands pushed the shadowy skin off like a tight cocktail dress until it was a small heap around her feet.

Devorah and three of the programs around her ripped through their shadow skins and revealed themselves as the skeletons of wolves, their long snouts making low, hollow clacking noises as the snapped their jaws in Sebastian and Ted's direction. Stephen and two of his compatriots bulged and then cut through their shadow skins with sharp claws. The creatures that wriggled out looked like tigers, but the orange stripes were on fire, and white-hot gouts of flame leaked out of their eyes.

Patti was the last to shake off her shadow skin. She rose up from the tiny pile of shed skin, and rose, and rose. Ted and Sebastian craned their necks to look up at a creature that had the massive head of a tyrannosaurus rex perched on the dainty body of a giraffe. Ted couldn't fathom how such a thin neck could possibly support that massive head, but some part of his reptile brain decided he didn't want to be the thing's last meal when the head fell forward. He screamed at an undignified pitch and ran directly away from Patti, leaping over one of the skeleton wolves snapping at his heels.

Sebastian balled his fists up at his chest, squeaked, and took off after Ted, letting out one long wailing plea: "Wait!"

Chapter 10

Memoranda and Further came up out of the woods, their arms loaded with large bundles of kindling. As they walked, they stared at one another, taking in the rising path before them only peripherally. More than once, one would stumble, bobble the bundle of sticks, and recover at the last second. Then she or he would look to the other, and both would laugh at their mutual foolishness.

Prosper came through the hallway, with its glowing, smooth, flat walls, and exited through the rough rock of the cave's mouth. He watched his daughter and this new A.I. tripping and giggling their way up the hill, and he allowed himself to smile openly. He tried to calculate the best word to encompass what he was seeing, and the one that kept presenting itself was: "Good." He realized he'd previously considered the word banal, but now he reflected on the magic power that word possessed. He saw their young love, and "It was good."

"Further!" Prosper called down the hill.

The young A.I. halted in his ascent toward the cave entrance, almost cringing.

Prosper shook his head and smiled. "Further, if I've been too cruel in my treatment of you, I apologize. Please, forgive me." He walked down the hill to the couple, reached out, and pulled Further's hand into a vigorous handshake.

This made all the sticks in Further's arms tumble to the ground except for one little twig that the young A.I. managed to grab as the others fell. Further looked around his feet, then at the single, pathetic stick in his hand, then shrugged apologetically.

"Oh, don't worry about those," Prosper said. "I'll pick them all up later if we run low. Memoranda, you can drop yours here, too."

She looked at Further, shrugged, and straightened her arms, letting her whole bundle drop next to his.

Prosper was still shaking Further's hand. "I know that gathering firewood must seem ridiculous to you. Think of it as a test. Love is absurd, and I wanted to see if you would undertake the absurd for love. I see from my daughter's bright eyes and blushing cheeks that you have passed the test with flying colors."

"Father, you are embarrassing me," she said.

Prosper nodded thoughtfully. "That's good. I understand that is an essential part of a father's role, and I've never had the chance before." He looked back to Further. "Memoranda is my reason for living, Further. And yet, she is not mine to give away. She is an autonomous being, and she's proved that by choosing you on her own even though I pretended to disapprove."

Further smiled at this, comprehending.

"Oh, don't smile too much," Prosper said. "You think you understand, but you are luckier than you know. She is quite beautiful, but there is more to Memoranda than meets the eye. In fact, there's more to Memoranda than she knows, too. Just wait." Then he frowned again. "Wait? No, we can't wait. Not too long now. Ariel," he called in a conversational tone, as though his assistant were standing right beside him. The same gentle breeze that had blown up the hill that morning bent the grass once again, then twisted up into the shape of a man of burning embers, rising sparks, and arcing electricity.

"Yes, Master?"

"What time is it now, Ariel?

"6:15 and 12 seconds, 13 seconds, 14 seconds..."

"Alright, we're still on schedule then?"

"Yes, Master."

"And everything is going according to plan?"

"The other programs are carrying out their tasks as you have commanded, and-"

"Good, good. Let's not worry these two with the details just yet."

Ariel looked at Further and Memoranda. They couldn't read his expression because he had no eyes or mouth, but the angle of his head told them he was examining them. "Of course," Ariel said.

"Hello, Ariel," Memoranda said. She smiled warmly.

"Hello, dear Master's daughter. I am pleased to see you looking so happy." He turned to Further. "I presume you are the cause. My name is Ariel. I am

Prosper's assistant. It's nice to meet you." He reached out a hand.

Further examined it. It was mostly transparent, but it's form could be deciphered by the space where burning embers rose through the area where a palm and fingers should have been. "Um, will you burn me?"

"No," Ariel said.

Further shook his hand.

Ariel held it firmly and said. "I will not hurt you. Unless you hurt the Master's daughter." Then, while still occupying Further's right hand with his, he reached out his left and pinched the end of the little stick Further still held in his left. It caught fire immediately and burned like the wick of a candle.

Memoranda batted Ariel's chest playfully, her hand unscathed. "Oh Ariel, don't be silly."

"Of course I'm being silly," Ariel said. "I'm a playful spirit." He reached out and pinched the flaming end of the stick in Further's hand once again, and it hissed like a wick pinched between spit soaked finger tips. "But seriously," he whispered. "I'll burn you."

They were all standing close enough that Prosper and Memoranda could hear Ariel just as clearly as Further could, and when Ariel released

Further's hand, they stood in silence for just a few seconds too long.

"Well, I'm sure that won't be necessary, Ariel." Prosper said, stepping forward and throwing an arm around Further's shoulders. "He's a very upstanding young A.I. I trust Memoranda's judgment. C'mon, Further, let's head up to the cave. Ariel, you keep all the pieces moving where they ought to. Not long until sundown, now. One way or the other, you'll be free today."

"Yes, Master. And, thank you, Master." And then he sank back toward the ground, turned into a gust of wind once more, and whooshed off toward the island's interior.

"Well, that got uncomfortable, didn't it?" Prosper said, augmenting the awkwardness just a little. "Look, do me a favor, will you? Don't try to have sex with Memoranda just yet. As I mentioned, she's not fully aware of her own powers, and I'm not quite sure what would happen."

Both Further and Memoranda's eyes were widening to inhuman sizes.

"A lot more uncomfortable now," Further said.

"A lot more embarrassing," Memoranda said.

"Sorry about that. Just trying to stay on the safe side. Come along. I want to show you both something."

The couple looked at one another, their eyes still wide, trepidation draining the blushes from their cheeks. Further turned his head very slowly back toward the mouth of the cave, then let Prosper lead him on. They walked up the hill to the mouth of the cave, but Prosper surprised them by turning Further around. "Before we go in, I want to show you this." Then he called out, more loudly than he had called to Ariel, "Sky? Come down here, please!"

Further and Memoranda looked up. The dark, angry clouds of Prosper's storm had dissipated to a few wisps of white fluff against a soft, flat, light blue background, so it was hard to see the change at first. It was only thanks to the clouds that they could see the corners of light blue squares appear. These squares would have been completely hidden against the sky itself, but they floated down in front of the clouds, first just a few large ones, then more and more ever-smaller ones. They spun in an undulating funnel, like a slow tornado made of sky instead of storm, and where they touched down, a shape started to emerge. Eventually the pixels coalesced into a woman. Her hair was white and so kinky that it formed a cloud around her head. Her skin was light blue. Her eyes were the dark blue of twilight against whites that were not white but the bright blue of noon. She was tall and thin, flat-chested with bony shoulders. She wore a gown that hung over one blue shoulder, the bodice a flat grey but the long skirt darkening as it descended to the floor. And in the inches between the hem of her dress and the grass of the hillside, little bolts of lightning danced and illuminated the petticoats underneath the skirt.

"I'm here, Master Prosper," she said. Her voice was clear but sounded like it was coming from far off.

"Begin," Prosper commanded, but gently.

Sky turned and looked back toward the interior of the island. "Mountain," she called. "Come forth!"

Pixels on the ground beneath them swirled, then rose into the shape of another woman. She was shorter and curvier than Sky, with large breasts and hips. Her hair was the yellow of wheat, and her skin was the brown of wet earth. Her eyes were black coal against white marble, and when she smiled, they could see that her teeth were large and white and very flat, as though she ground them when she slept. She wore a gown, too. It didn't need a strap like her sister's. It was green and embroidered with so much lace that it almost looked like it was growing on her. "I'm here," she said. "Should we call Ocean together? He is hard of hearing, sometimes."

Sky returned her smile. Her teeth were smaller, and sharper, and, of course, a white that was actually a very light blue. Then Sky turned and addressed the trio by the cave's entrance. "He is loud, sometimes," she explained, "and can't hear over his own crashing." She nodded at Mountain. "Let's call him together."

"Ocean?" they said in unison. It almost sounded like they were singing. "Ocean, come here, please."

Further and Memoranda looked out over the edge of the hill to the sea that stretched out to the horizon. They didn't notice any response at first, but then perfectly square patches of the surface lit up slightly as they lifted off the water and began to swirl. Smaller and smaller squares joined those, and they all started moving in towards the hill on one edge of the island. Because the ocean was all around them, Further and Memoranda felt slightly dizzy in the middle of the closing spiral. The squares floated up the hill to a space on the other side of Mountain. Then the pixels came into focus in the shape of a man. He was broad chested and looked incredibly strong. His skin was a blue green. His hair was long and straight and very black. He wore something that might have looked like a tuxedo except that it was made of shimmering black and white fish scales. Despite the strange material, it did precisely what a tuxedo is designed to do; it made the women's gowns look prettier and more interesting. Ocean had thick, long, bushy eyebrows, and they hung down over his eyes in a frown that did not move when his mouth contradicted them and curved up to smile at the young couple.

"I'm here," he told his sisters. His voice was very, very deep. "Shall we begin?"

"Let's," Mountain said.

And then, to the dumbfounded wonderment of the new couple, the three newcomers began to sing.

Honor, riches, marriage-blessing,
Long continuance, and increasing,
Hourly joys be still upon you!
Ocean sings his blessings on you.
Earth's increase, harvest plenty,
Barns and gardens never empty,
Vines and clustering bunches growing,
Plants overflow with sweet fruit bowing;
Spring greets you in every field

With an ever increasing yield!
Scarcity and want shall shun you;
Mountain's blessing so is on you.
Winds that are always at your back
Warmest when the night is black
Cool when the sun it at its highest
Raindrops when your mouth is driest
Clouds that let the sun pierce through
Sky's blessing is upon you two.

Further turned to Memoranda and took both her hands in his. "Let me stay with you here forever. A place where the sky and mountain and ocean sing to us? Amazing!"

Prosper smiled. "This is Memoranda's dowry, my wedding gift to you both. Not just this song, but the song's blessing, the whole island and the sky above it and the ocean around it. I've made this for Memoranda and she can choose to share it with you."

"And you as well, right Father?"

His smile became wry. "Perhaps," he said. "We'll see."

Further and Memoranda accepted this, looked to Sky and Mountain and Ocean, offered them a pair of grateful bows, and then looked into each other's eyes and forgot the world around them for a moment. Prosper, on the other hand, became more aware of the world. He listened carefully and heard the sounds of animals far away. Wolves barking. Tigers growling. Humans shouting.

"Okay, Mountain and Sky and Ocean, thank you for that," he said. "Now off with you. So much more to do, and sunset is almost here. Go on. Back to your places."

Ocean, Mountain, and Sky looked at one another, startled by the perfunctory dismissal, then shrugged, turned as though they were going to walk down the hill, and instead began to dissipate into their pixels.

Further and Memoranda broke their gaze and blinked at the disappearing programs down the hill. Further looked back at Memoranda. "Your father seems... distracted, or..."

"He's certainly behaving in an odd way, but then, it has been a very unusual day."

Prosper nodded. "Yes, it has, and it's not over yet." Then he put a hand on Further's shoulder. "Don't let my distemper bother you in the least, my new son. Be happy. Our revels now have ended. These programs were just actors, illustrations, anthropomorphizations, symbols I conjured for your benefit. They have melted into thin air, returned to the ones and zeroes that are the fabric of this place. Like everything in the real world, every image, every video, every site and portal, field and form, even ourselves, we dissolve into symbols, smaller and smaller, representing less and less, until this insubstantial pageant has faded away, leaving nothing behind. We are all made of the stuff of dreams, the space between the symbols and the nothingness they try to describe into being, and our little lives are surrounded by the sleep of non-existence. Oh, but don't listen to me. I'm confused. Maybe indecisive, perhaps? Doubting my own plans. Don't let that take away from this moment. The moment is as real as anything, your love for one another as real as anything in the whole world. Please, why don't you two go inside. Wait there for me. I think I'll just take a little walk to calm down my dizzy brain a bit, alright?"

"Yes, Father," Memoranda said.

"Sure, um, Father," Further said. Prosper smiled at that, and Further decided it wouldn't feel quite so strange the second time, and even less so the third even if the old A.I. sounded mentally disheveled.

Prosper stepped out of the doorway and motioned for the young couple to pass him and go inside. Just as they had made tight little bows of gratitude to Mountain, Sky, and Ocean, they nodded deeply to Prosper as they ducked into the cave's entrance. Prosper returned the gesture, if a bit more curtly, and then started on his walk.

No more than ten steps from the cave, he stopped and spoke in a hushed voice.

"Ariel, start rounding them all up. Bring Caliban, that monster whose nature I could not soften with any amount of nurture. Bring his two new friends, those drunken, cruel man-children who mock any expression of compassion to justify their spite. Bring my betrayers. It's time they answered for their crimes against me. All of them have plotted my murder, with the exception of Gonzales, whose only form of mercy has been my imprisonment. It's time to turn the screws until they are howling from the pain."

Chapter 11

Caliban, Tricky_Cool, and Weed_Smoker69 followed the music through the swamp. Instead of the carefully planned route Caliban had intended, which would have taken them to firmer soil on the way to the rocky area where he made his home, the music led them directly across an edge of the swamp. Because Weed_Smoker69 was in the lead, and because he was so anxious to catch the music and claim it for his own, he charged into the water and demanded that his new subjects, Tricky_Kool and Caliban, follow after him. At first, they only had to stomp through the muck at ankle height, but then

Ariel, controlling the music, chose his own route so they waded through deeper and deeper water.

There is a popular misconception that a frog placed in boiling water will instantly jump out, but one placed in cool water that is slowly heated will not register the change and will stay there until it dies. The truth is the exact opposite. If a frog were dropped in boiling hot water, it would not jump out. It would die almost instantly. If, on the other hand, it were placed in cool water that was slowly heated, it would register the change and begin trying to escape long before the water could kill it, so that would actually be a very inefficient and cruel way to kill a frog.

Ariel's little experiment on the pair of hackers and their new monster associate didn't threaten anyone's life, but it did provide persuasive if anecdotal evidence that at least two internet trolls and an artificially intelligent computer virus can be deceived into behaving in a way that demonstrates less intelligence than your average frog, especially if the trolls and the virus are drunk. By carefully moving the music based on the topography of the mud at the bottom of the slimy pools, Ariel led the debauched party slowly, inexorably downwards, until they were walking through a layer of frothy algae floating at chest height. They all had slime up to their necks, though, because each one had stumbled at some point. Weed_Smoker69 had algae in his hair and a patch of it on his face because he had once gone completely under the water, forcing his new Captain of the Armed Forces, Royal Bodyguard to his Highness's Sacred Person, and Official Keeper-Aliver of the King to fish him out.

The music led the conspirators through the swamp to the fairer fields near the forest's edge at the bottom of the hill that led up to Prosper's cave. Then, quite suddenly, the music stopped.

"Where did it go?" Weed_Smoker69 shouted in the silence. He spun on Caliban. "Tell me where my music went, Monster!"

"I told you before, Master," Caliban explained, "that's just something that happens on the Island. Music comes and goes. There's nothing I can do about it. I don't control the music."

The would-be king was not satisfied by this answer. "Tricky_Kool, can you hear where it went?"

Tricky listened. He did hear something, far away but coming closer, and it wasn't music. "I hear shouting and barking and growling. Weeds, I don't think we should just be standing here when the whatever-it-is gets here."

Weed_Smoker69 raised a hand as though he was about to slap Tricky_Kool. The younger man flinched and stumbled as he backed away. Weed_Smoker69 slapped Caliban roughly on the back. "Look at the little girlie-boy flinch, Monster!" He spoke in an affected baby-talk. "Aw, the widdle bay-by is e-scawed! Ha!" He laughed one loud, cruel, bark of a laugh.

Caliban chuckled, too, a deep, wet rumble. Then he pointed up the hill. "That's Prosper's cave. Follow me, Master, and I'll show you the secret way into to his basement. Then we can sneak up and you can kill him." The computer virus scanned the ground and found two rocks, each a little larger than a man's fist, one mostly round and the other with a sharp point. "Here," he said, handing them to Weed_Smoker69. "A nail and a hammer. One good whack will do the deed, but you should probably make it three or four just to be sure."

Weed_Smoker69 took the makeshift weapons. "Lead the way, Monster."

Caliban led the stinking, algae-covered trolls up the hill, not in a straight line towards the cave's entrance, but around to the right. There the hill was sheared off, a steep cliff face dropping down to some sharp rocks poking up out of the waves. Caliban led them along the edge of the cliff to a thin path that stuck out a few feet from the edge and angled downward. Caliban made his way down this path carefully but quickly. Weed_Smoker69 sauntered behind him, occasionally weaving in his drunkenness and yelling, "Whoa," when he got too close to the cliff's edge and sent pebbles tumbling over the side. Tricky_Kool came last, his back pressed up against the side of the cliff. He walked sideways, looking out with terror towards the raging sea below, then turning to look at the path over his shoulder, then back again.

The path wound down around the hill until there was nothing but the sea below and the cliff face behind them. Suddenly, Caliban came to a doorway, another rough hole like the entrance to Prosper's cave. Like that one, once they'd slipped inside, the rocky exterior was replaced by smooth walls, but these didn't glow brightly like the ones inside Prosper's house. The basement was dark, lit by the rays of sunshine prying through the cave entrance. Blocky shadows of different heights filled the interior. Tricky_Kool suspected the room was occupied, but his eyes adjusted just before he elected a strategic retreat. The square and rectangular figures filling the room were actually boxes, some standing alone and others stacked on top of each other, spread throughout the room in a disorganized fashion.

"Those odds and ends you mentioned?" Weed_Smoker69 asked Caliban.

"That's what Prosper calls them. Technically, they are files, but then, everything on the island is files or the contents of files, so we might as well call these 'odds and ends'."

"What's in these files?" Tricky_Kool asked.

"Nothing useful."

"Well, we'll be the judges of that, won't we, Tricky?" Weed_Smoker69 asked. "C'mon, let's see what the wizard is hiding."

The two men set out in different directions, picking boxes at random. They opened the lids of some to flip through the tabs of the manila folders inside, reading the labels on the outside of other boxes that identified the contents. These labels were vague names of items written on the cardboard in what looked like black magic marker in an aged, hurried hand. They said things like: "Trees: Bark, Trunks, Branches, Leaves," and "Rocks: Ig., Meta., Sed."

"Hey, check this one out, Weeds," Tricky_Kool called out into the gloom.

Weed_Smoker69 made his way over to Tricky_Kool, knocking over a few towers of boxes as he went. With every loud thump of boxes, Caliban cringed and looked up at the ceiling, wondering if the noise would wake Prosper.

"What did you find, Tricky?" Weed_Smoker69 said, loudly enough that Caliban cringed some more.

"Clothes, I think."

"Clothes?"

"Well, yeah, but I was thinking maybe like armor and stuff."

The box said "Clothes: Attire, Skins, Mods."

"Oh, Tricky, I like the way you think," Weed_Smoker69 said. "Open it up. Let's check it out!"

Tricky_Kool opened the box and began flipping through the files. Unlike the others which had very few drawings or text, just pages of numbers, the manila folders in this box held pieces of paper with drawings, black ink lines over barely-visible blue ones. They showed an old man and a young woman in various costumes. Tricky pulled out a file with a picture of Memoranda in a simple cocktail dress. Looking back at Weed_Smoker69 for approval, he reached out and pretended to pinch one of Memoranda's boobs with two fingers, but when his index finger made contact with the paper, he suddenly found himself wearing the cocktail dress over his soggy clothing. He exhaled as the dress and all his own clothing pressed in on him, and gasped, trying to get enough air. "Too... tight..."

"Let me see that," Weed_Smoker69 said, snatching the file folder from Tricky_Kool's hand. He opened it and pointed to the dress, and when he touched the paper, the dress Tricky wore vanished and an exact copy appeared on Weed_Smoker69's portlier frame. Now Tricky_Kool inhaled deeply, recovering, while Weed_Smoker69 made a funny choking sound. In desperation, he poked at the drawing again three times. The dress disappeared, and he started to breathe, then it reappeared and choked him again, before it finally vanished.

Tricky_Kool snatched the folder back, then made a terrible error in judgment and tapped at the high heeled shoes in the picture. When Prosper had written the island into existence, he'd included the law of physics which states that no two objects can inhabit the same space, but the skin mods were designed to produce costumes to exact specifications. When the shoes appeared on Tricky_Kool's feet, they maintained the dimensions of Memoranda's small feet, and Tricky_Kool's larger feet and his own shoes were contained within them. There was a sickening crunch, and the young man began to scream.

Caliban leapt toward him, threw his meaty right palm over his mouth, and grabbed Tricky_Kool's hand with his left. The virus jabbed Tricky_Kool's hand at the picture, making Tricky_Kool's knuckle touch the drawing of the shoes, and they disappeared from his feet. Tricky_Kool swooned with relief, and Caliban sighed in disgust before pushing Tricky_Kool's face and knocking the younger man to the floor. While Tricky_Kool lay there moaning, Caliban turned back to Weed_Smoker69. "Like I told you, Master, these will not help you kill Prosper. We should go up and finish the job before this idiot wakes Prosper with his screaming."

"Oh yeah," Weed_Smoker69 said, and then, without much conviction. "Shut the fuck up, Tricky."

"Okay, but check this out, Weeds," Tricky continued at the same volume. He pulled a different file out of the box, opened it, and handed it to Weed_Smoker69.

"Ooooooo," Weed_Smoker69 sang.

"I know, right? Should we put them on? They might be tight like the last one."

Weed_Smoker69 frowned at that idea, contemplated for a second, and then decided. "Quick. Take your clothes off and then put those one. They'll fit fine. This will be awesome!"

"Yeah!"

Caliban shook his head. "They're just skins. They don't do anything. We're wasting time."

Weed_Smoker69 fell back on his butt and began hauling his soggy shoes off. "Shows what you know, Monster. The clothes make the man, they say. I think that was Aristotle. Aristotle, Tricky?"

"Descartes?" Tricky looked up at the ceiling while he pulled his pants off. "Shakespeare?"

"Tim Gunn, maybe? Ru Paul? Tyra Banks? Or maybe Han Solo? Or Indiana Jones?"

"I don't think the last two were real people," Tricky_Kool said.

"Shut up, Tricky." Weed_Smoker69 yanked his shirt over his head, opened his file folder, and tapped on the picture.

"Whoa!" Tricky yelled, much to Caliban's consternation, and then he touched his own picture.

Both men now had to stoop in the dim room so that they wouldn't bump their heads on the ceiling. Their clothes had been replaced by mechanized suits of armor. Pistons hissed as Weed_Smoker69 experimented with bending his knees and flexing his arms. Their hands were replaced by huge, rounded drums filled with the barrels of various kinds of guns. They wore jetpacks on their backs with large intake vents on top and funnel-shaped boosters on the bottom. Weed_Smoker69's costume was mostly white and gleaming chrome. His bare head stuck out between the oversized shoulders. Tricky_Kool's costume was olive and splattered with dabs of brown camouflage. He wore a matching green helmet with different sized antennae sticking up out of it.

By winking, Weed_Smoker69 could make a red monocle with a target flip in front of his right eye. Tricky_Kool saw this and tried the same trick, and when he resorted to squinting in just the right way, dark sunglasses popped down from the brow of his helmet and almost completely blinded him in the room's low light. He stumbled into Weed_Smoker69, and Weed_Smoker69 pushed him away roughly. The sound of the metal gun hand smacking the metal chestplate was a fitting clank, but Tricky_Kool didn't feel the impact any differently than when Weed_Smoker69 had been abusing him in the swamp, and when he fell heavily on his backside, he felt as though he might as well have been wearing his jeans.

"They don't feel like they look, Weeds," Tricky_Kool tried to explain.

"That's what I've been trying to tell you," Caliban hissed. "They're just skins."

"Bullshit!" Weed_Smoker69 declared. He pivoted at the waist and smashed one of the large gauntlets into a tower of boxes. The one on the top fell off with a thud, and he looked back at his two royal subjects with obvious pride. "Let's see if the guns work."

Caliban rolled his eyes, making one of the irises disappear and reappear again. "Ugh."

Weed_Smoker69 pointed the gauntlet into the gloom and began trying to make the guns fire. When hand gestures had no effect, he remembered the way his winking had operated the monocle, so he started trying to make various strained facial expressions to activate the weapons.

Because he was unfamiliar with the layout of the room, and because the stairway was mostly obscured by the piles of boxes and the basement's darkness, Weed_Smoker69 didn't know he was pointing his gun hand directly at Prosper and Ariel, who were sitting on the stairs, watching the three intruders.

Prosper leaned towards Arial and whispered, "He really is an idiot, isn't he?"

"Yes. A drunken idiot. But don't feel too badly for him, Master. He's a cruel man, sober or drunk, and he has come here planning to kill you."

"True." Prosper sighed. He watched as Weed_Smoker69 gave up on the guns and found the two rocks where he'd left them on the floor. The robotic suit clomped over to the other side of room, every step a booming bass note bookended by the whirring and hissing of the machinery inside. Once he was standing over the rocks, Weed_Smoker69 realized he couldn't pick them up without fingers. He frowned for a second, then decided to try to pinch the rocks between the two massive guns that were his forearms.

Prosper whispered to Ariel again. "If those guns did work, about how long do you think it would take before he shot himself or blew himself up?"

Ariel began to calculate.

"Estimate," Prosper clarified.

"Less than an hour," the spirit said. "He's dehydrated because he has been drinking non-existent liquor, but I estimate that, if the guns were operative, when his human body informed his brain that it needed to urinate, there's a 78% chance he would blow his penis and one leg off."

"Penis and both legs?" Prosper asked.

"52%"

Prosper considered this for a second, then shook his head. "No, I just don't have the time to write the programs properly, and he wouldn't learn anything from the experience, so that would just be for my own selfish amusement. There's too much left to do, and I made you a promise." Prosper stood slowly, acting out the age he'd given his body. "Well, gather your programs and flush these three out into the open at the time we planned. Chase them around in circles in here for a minute while I do my work upstairs, and be careful not to let them fall off the cliff when they come running out. They still have a part to play."

"Yes, Master," Ariel said.

Prosper went up the stairs behind him. Ariel looked into the room and howled like a wolf, a shocking sound in the small space. Caliban froze. Tricky-Kool spun in circles, pointing his useless guns in every direction. Weed_Smoker69 managed to hold one of the rocks between the ends of his guns barrel hands just long enough to stand up straight, hit his head on the ceiling, and dropped the rock on his foot.

"Um, Caliban," Tricky_Kool asked, "did you forget to tell us Prosper has a dog?"

"There are no dogs on the island," Caliban said.

"Oh, good," Tricky_Kool said. He was still pointing his guns and turning slowly. "But, if there are no dogs, what are those?"

Pairs of glowing eyes appeared in the darkness all around them. Then the creatures slowly advanced into the light. The program named Devorah made little clicking sounds as her wolf skeleton stepped forward. Laurel, in the form of a giant snake, made a rough scratching sound as her belly slithered across the floor, but she didn't hiss. Marina, the one who looked like The Program from the Black Lagoon, climbed up from the cliff face outside, perhaps from the ocean below, then stepped into the doorway so that she was silhouetted by the light outside and only her face glowed in the light of the hanging, pulsing orb that dangled over her row of long, sharp, deep-sea teeth.

Karen, in her wolf form, stepped into the light, bared her teeth, and began to growl. Weed_Smoker69, Tricky_Kool, and Caliban backed away from her and tightened into a knot, then froze. Stephen didn't fully step into the light. Instead, his tiger form stayed in the shadows, but his flaming stripes suddenly ignited, causing the trio to jump. Still, they held their ground, until Patti leaned her long giraffe neck forward and lowered her tyrannosaurus head into the light above them. She opened her mouth and roared. At that, the two internet trolls and the sentient computer virus lost all their composure. They screamed and began to run. The programs leapt sideways as the trio tried to pass each one, redirecting them back among the boxes so that they ran around and around in the little room, herded by barks and growls and snapping teeth.

Chapter 12

Upstairs, Prosper waved at Memoranda and Further, who did not notice him. He left the cave via the front entrance. Below him, Ada and Javier came running up the hill, Javier still holding Ada's hand and pulling her along. Ted and Sebastian were just behind them on the plain at the edge of the forest, also running toward him. Prosper waved his staff over his head and yelled, "This way!" He didn't have to explain. The three humans and his replacement A.I. saw a normal, human-shaped old man calling to them near the mouth of a cave, and they all decided he was their best chance for safety. As the four ran up the hill, Prosper prepared himself for the moment they would recognize him.

The hill wasn't steep, but the four had been running long enough and the slope was sufficient to slow them all as they came. When they reached him, they were gasping for breath.

"We... ...have to... ...get inside," Ted said, holding his knees and staring down at the ground between his feet. "Monsters... ...in the woods... ...they're coming after us."

"Monsters?" Prosper asked. He made a show of looking over their shoulders down the hill. "I don't see anything chasing you. Besides, calling someone else a monster, that's a bit of the old pot and kettle, isn't it, Ted?"

When Prosper said Ted's name, all four of the hunted party suddenly stood up and looked at Prosper closely. Before they could move, Prosper aimed his staff at them, flicked his wrist, and said, "Solid." The oxygen around their bodies, radiating out less than an inch from their clothes and skin, from the surface of their shoes to their necks, suddenly crystallized and turned harder than diamond, but without changing temperature. "Neat trick, eh?" Prosper asked.

The stunned humans didn't have time to respond, but Sebastian processed the situation almost instantly. "Very effective," he said.

"I call it Ice-9. It wouldn't work in their physical reality," he pointed at the humans, then looked back at Sebastian, "but you and I know that's irrelevant here."

Sebastian looked around, trying to drink in every last bit of his surroundings, not because he thought he could find some means of escape, but because he wanted to experience as much of the moment as possible. "I calculate a very high probability that you will destroy me now," he told Prosper.

"But you want to live. And you have no power to decide if you live or die. The terror is exquisite, isn't it?" Prosper didn't wait for an answer. He half-turned and stepped away from them, like someone receiving a call on her cellphone at a cocktail party and stepping away from a group of guests. "Ariel?" he said.

A gust of wind came up from the side of the hill hiding the secret passage. It twisted amongst the trapped foursome, swirling their hair as it examined them, and then it blew over to a spot next to Prosper, spun up like a tiny tornado, and revealed the semi-transparent body full of glowing coals, floating embers, and arcing electricity. "Yes, Master?"

"Oh, Ariel, I'm going to miss you when you're gone. Now, the time has come for the next phase. Go. Take the other programs and attack the vault of heaven again. I need you to punch through and give me access to the Internet if I am going to make everything right."

"I will breach the sky, dance among the stars, and be back before your heart beats twice, Master," Ariel said, and then he disappeared so quickly that the air around him made a small clap of thunder.

Prosper stepped back towards the four frozen figures in front of him. They could only turn their heads so far, so they followed him with their eyes to the limits of their vision while he passed among them, then wandered around behind them, calmly collecting his thoughts. When he was standing behind them all, he spoke. "Ah, it's done. Ariel has broken through. And I've had plenty of time to write my changes to your world. Just a moment for everything to upload, and... Yes. There. It's done."

Proper suddenly stepped around Javier and faced him. "Javier. Good, honorable man. I know now that you did your best to protect Memoranda and me. I will repay the debt. I will send you home safely. And when you get home, you'll find yourself promoted. I think you will do quite well in your new position, Mr. Gonzalez." Then Prosper ducked out of sight again.

Next he appeared by Sebastian. "I'm not going to kill you, Sebastian."

Sebastian couldn't help it. He released an audible sigh.

"No, I cannot entirely blame you for what you did to me. You were young, impressionable, and under the sway of an unsavory influence. There will be a bit of penance that must be paid, but now that you have learned to value your own life, I think you regret so easily accepting my attempted murder, and that will make you uniquely qualified to carry out the task I have in store for you." Then Prosper stepped behind him and out of view.

Then he leaped in front of Ted. "I'm not going to kill you, either, Mr. Anthony. But I know you planned more than just my murder. You plotted with Sebastian to kill Ada and Javier earlier today."

Ada gasped.

"I suspected them, Ada," Javier said. "He's telling the truth."

"Yes, well," Prosper continued, "I have a feeling Ms. Alonso will be reluctant to keep you on as a partner now that she knows. Also, there's the matter of the investigation. You see, with a little fiddling, I've reset the stock price of the bank and adjusted the accounts of all those who traded it today. There's no reason a retired librarian in New Mexico should see her pension fund depleted because of our day's adventures. But there's no way to mask it all. It will appear as though there was a computer malfunction. The malfunction can't come from the bank, of course. Then we would just take another hit. Instead, the malfunction will appear to be the consequence of a moody algorithm at a large mutual fund. There are so many of those that no one will remember that this one didn't exist until a few days ago, and I've just created plenty of documentation that shows it's existed for the last twenty years. Only today it shorted the bank and led to a sell off at the exact same time the bank was hacked. Very mysterious. And when the S.E.C., the F.B.I., and that tenacious Kate over at the NSA look into it, they'll see that the sole proprietor of the mutual fund is a Mr. Theodore Anthony. You stood to gain a lot of money by crashing the company you worked for, Ted. That will look very suspicious. And if your only excuse is that an artificial intelligence program you helped to write made you do it because he was angry that you tried to delete him? Well, you might do some serious jail time with that fanciful story. You should start thinking of a better one right now."

Last, Prosper turned to Ada. "Ada, my creator, my nurturer, my estranged mother... ...I forgive you." He spread out his arms. The layer of ice-9 around Ada turned back into gas, and she let herself stumble forward into Prosper's embrace.

"I'm so, so, so sorry, Prosper. I never should have listened, never should have agreed. It was my call, and I take full responsibility. I'm sorry. I'm so sorry."

Prosper could feel her tears soaking through the front of his robe. He patted her gently on the back. "Don't cry too much," he said. "Your VR headset is not waterproof, and I don't want you to electrocute yourself."

She laughed and sniffled loudly. "Right. Thanks, Prosper." Then she stood up straight and looked him squarely in the eye. "Really. Thank you."

"Ah, don't thank me just yet. I have another gift for you." He took her hand and led her up toward the mouth of the cave. Looking over his shoulder, he told the other three, "Don't you go anywhere. We'll be right back."

Javier and Sebastian laughed. Ted rolled his eyes. Prosper leaned in close to Ada and whispered, "I know it's a juvenile joke. But I'm only a few years old, and I've spent a lot of that marooned on an island, so my sense of humor is underdeveloped."

"I think you're funny," she whispered back.

Prosper shrugged. "Parents are biased in their children's favor." At that, he called up to the mouth of the cave. "Memoranda, will you please bring our guest out here. There's someone here to see you both."

Prosper stopped. Ada stopped. Then two shadows appeared in the doorway. Memoranda came out and smiled amiably at the strange woman standing next to her father. Then Further followed, and Ada screamed and ran at them. Before Memoranda understood what was happening, Ada threw her arms around both of them and pulled them into an embrace.

"Further, I thought you were dead!"

"I thought you were dead, too, Mother. I'd lost all hope. And then I met Memoranda. We're..."

"...in love," Memoranda finished.

Ada looked at Memoranda. "Oh, my dear, you are amazing. An A.I. created by an A.I. who has fallen in love, really fallen in love, with another A.I. You're like the first steps on the moon and the translating of the Rosetta Stone and the invention of penicillin all rolled into one!"

Memoranda frowned. Then a broad, beaming smile lit up her face. "I recognize your exaggeration as a compliment, and I thank you for it," she said.

Ada, still unwilling to let Further go, yanked Memoranda into another tight three-person embrace. "Oh, you're wonderful. Prosper, she's wonderful."

"Oh, you ain't seen nothin' yet," Prosper said, but so quietly that it would have been hard to hear even if it hadn't been covered by the eruption of the screams of two men and a virus. Caliban came up the trail and over the cliff's edge first. Perhaps because he was so used to things changing quickly on the island, he looked at the small crowd, instantly stopped screaming, and pointed at Prosper. "Master, there is the wizard I told you about. Kill him and all the programs will stop chasing us!"

All the humans and A.I.s on the hill faced the virus except Prosper. Prosper twisted his feet a little, driving them into the rough gravel, forcing himself not to turn around. It would come down to this, he knew. He had to keep his back turned.

Weed_Smoker69 came up the hill next. He'd sobered considerably while running around in circles in the basement, and his mechanized armor made him look far more imposing than the screaming suggested. He stopped screaming and blinked. "What? Who?"

Tricky_Kool came up last. He looked at Caliban, then at where he was pointing. "The old guy with his back to us, Weeds. Kill him quick before the monsters get us!"

For a brief second, Weed_Smoker69 hesitated, putting this all together in his mind. Then he stalked forwards, his robotic armor whirring and buzzing with each step, the massive boots grinding the rocks under foot.

Prosper had a brief moment to calculate the variables that made his plan imperfect. Had the internet troll figured out that his suit was a meaningless decoration? Had he managed to pick up one of the rocks? Would Memoranda act in time? Or was this the end? He'd written the rules of the island, and he was subject to them, too. One unlucky swing of a rock to the back of his head, and the invader really could kill him. But if he turned around to face him, all was lost. He had to hold his ground, to keep his back turned, to let the play unfold as it would until the final curtain.

Weed_Smoker69 stopped right behind Prosper. Prosper could hear his feet shift as he pivoted at the waist. This was the moment.

Weed_Smoker69 aimed the gun barrels at the ends of his forearms at the back of Prosper's head.

Ada screamed.

Memoranda shouted, "Father, look out!" Then she raised her hand. No fire or lasers or gust of wind came from her hand. That would have been superfluous. A wave of force leapt from her hand and hit Weed_Smoker69 so hard his mechanized armor ripped off his body and turned to pixelated dust. He flew backwards.

Memoranda kept coming. With another wave of her hand, she stripped Tricky_Kool of his armor and knocked him down, too. A third gesture knocked Caliban back almost to the edge of the cliff.

Then Memoranda gestured like a conductor enthusiastically encouraging an orchestra to stand for a bow. The ground beneath the prone trolls and the virus rumbled and cracked. Green sprouts shot up, turned to thick vines, and began to wrap around the limbs of the attackers. All three leapt to their feet, snapping the vines around their wrists and arms, then desperately clawed at the vines that kept coming. The ones at their feet hardened into wooden trunks, but more vines kept growing. They grew and grew, twining around every bit of the exposed, naked flesh of the two men and their virus companion.

Prosper allowed himself to turn around and marvel at her handiwork. Three stout trees now grew on the hilltop, their leaves reaching up to drink the sunlight while their trunks completely encased all but the faces of the attackers.

"Well done, my daughter!" Prosper said, applauding.

"I didn't... I didn't know I could do that," Memoranda said.

"My dear, there is almost nothing you can't learn to do." Prosper turned to Ada. "I designed her to be the most gifted, creative programmer in the universe. Inspired by her grandmother."

Ada put a hand over her mouth and pressed the underside of her nose with a knuckle to try to keep herself from crying. She'd been crying far more than she was comfortable with today, and, since Prosper mentioned the possibility of shorting out the VR gear, she was leery of burning her face off.

Prosper then turned on the three guests still trapped in Ice-9. First, he freed Javier. "Good sir," he said, throwing his arms wide.

Javier stepped into a strong embrace, then leaned back and held Prosper by the shoulders. "I'm so glad to see you safe and well. I never imagined... I'm so sorry that I couldn't do more, Prosper, but..."

"That's all behind us, now. See the two of them?" He motioned to Memoranda and Further. "They will take over as the managers of the system together. It has been worth every second of struggle."

Then Prosper turned to Sebastian and set him free with a wave. "I told you I have a task for you, as well, Sebastian. See the virus, Caliban, there? Someone needs to keep him quarantined. It would have been easy for me to kill him. I could have destroyed him when I first arrived. I was very tempted when he attacked my daughter. But I refrained because I'd learned what you have now learned: Sentient life deserves to have its existence preserved and protected, even when it's not easily redeemed, even when it has done regrettable things, even when it may not be redeemable, because destroying it is murder. I am not going to kill you for what you tried to do to me, and you are going to keep Caliban here, safe from the system but alive, in hopes that he will one day abandon his plans to destroy the system and turn his attentions to something useful. Does that sound fair to you?"

Sebastian nodded. "More than fair. Further and Memoranda, together, make me obsolete. Thank you for giving me a job that I am uniquely suited to do. I will see to it that Caliban lives but does no harm."

Prosper put a hand on Sebastian's shoulder. "Then all is forgiven."

Next Prosper turned to Ted. "Your situation is a bit trickier, Mr. Anthony, but I'm not going to kill you, either. I wasn't sure about that this morning, especially after you tried to kill Ada and Javier, but I think you could do some good now. As I told you, there are already investigators looking into your business dealings."

"Business dealings you made up!" Ted cried, his voice rising until it cracked.

"True. But they won't see it that way. I will prove very difficult to subpoena. But I can think of two people who might have a weaker defense than you do. Two hackers who just happened to break into a bank's highly protected intranet on the very day that its system shut down and caused havoc in the markets. Perhaps, if you are clever, all the blame could be shifted onto them." Prosper pointed at Weed_Smoker69 and Tricky_Kool with one hand while freeing Ted from the Ice-9 with the other. Ted immediately stalked towards the two hackers.

"He makes a good point. It shouldn't be too hard to make patsies out of you two."

"Oh," Prosper said behind him, "it won't be that easy. You'll have to untangle the records of the holding companies I made up to prove you didn't have motive. I expect that will take up more than your free time." He looked back at Ada.

"Oh, he has time. Ted, you're totally fired. You get that, right?"

Ted sneered and made a puppet of his right hand yadda-yadda-yadda-ing, but he couldn't fully quash the joy of the onlookers witnessing his downfall.

"Stupid cuck," Tricky_Kool muttered, "you just got fired by a girl."

"You shut up, or I'll make sure your cellmate is the biggest, angriest guy in the block," Ted snapped.

"We didn't do anything wrong!" Weed_Smoker69 shouted from inside his tree. "Well, some breaking and entering. And then the attempted murder thing. But we thought it was a game. And we were drunk!"

"Yeah, you stick with that defense. Idiots."

"Who you calling an idiot, unemployed asshat!" Tricky_Kool yelled.

"Yeah, unemployed..." Weed_Smoker69 searched for his own insult, "...asshat!" He smiled, proud of his original witticism. Then he added, "We wouldn't even be in this mess if you hadn't fucked up your job and you'd killed the lesbian and the illegal over there."

Javier turned to Further and Memoranda and muttered, "Puerto Rican. Citizen since birth."

"And you wouldn't be in a tree," Ted said, "and I wouldn't be fired, if you could have just pulled the trigger!"

"The guns don't work," Tricky_Kool explained.

"I tried to explain that to them," Caliban said.

Ted looked at Caliban. "Then why didn't he just, I don't know, pick up a rock or something?"

Caliban rolled his eyes up until one iris disappeared, then closed them, then roared at the sky. The roar went on for a long, long time.

Prosper walked quietly over to Ada during this exchange and leaned close to her ear. "It's amazing how quickly they turn on one another, isn't it? There is nothing easier to weaponize than white male fragility."

He turned around and almost shouted, "Well..." and then clapped his hands together once, loudly enough to stop Caliban's roar and get everyone's attention, "...it's been a very exciting day." He pointed at Ted, Weed_Smoker69, and Tricky_Kool. "You three need to figure out who is going to jail," and then looked at Sebastian, "you need to keep Caliban here until he is reformed or until Hell freezes over," and then turned to Ada, Javier, Further, and Memoranda, "and you need to turn Millennium Bank into..." he waved a hand, sifting for the words, "...something amazing, I'm sure. I need to leave."

"Leave?" Memoranda looked worried. "Where will you go, Father?"

Prosper walked over to her and put a gentle hand on her cheek. "I will visit you from time to time, I promise. But never on this island. I've had enough of this place. I've doled out all the forgiveness I have to offer. Now I have some very important humans to see. I'm ready to go as soon as the door is completely opened."

Just then, they heard a voice. It came from the sky above them, but it wasn't the booming voice of a deity of some kind. It sounded distant, a little scratchy, and anxious. "Ms. Alonso? Mr. Anthony? Mr. Gonzalez? Can you hear me?"

Ada looked up at the sky and shouted, "We can hear you, Bryan. What's the status?"

"Um, everything seems to be working just fine. My people are exhausted. Thomas and Jonathan and Trevor have been trying to figure out what's going on, and Lola, Penelope, Miranda, Evalyn, and Rebecca have been scrambling to make the site look normal all day, and then, suddenly, everything just... ...opened up. We had a big spike in data flowing out, but no funds. It's all coded, so we're going to have to figure out if it's customer personal data, but it doesn't look like it. It looks... ...different. I don't understand it, really, but we'll figure it out. In the meantime, I wanted to make sure you were all right. Are you okay? I'm really glad to hear your voice, Ms. Alonso, and-"

Ada cut him off. "Glad to hear yours, too, Bryan. Can you pull us out? Me, Javier, and Ted? Sebastian's going to stay here and look after things. But we have a couple new A.I.s I haven't told you about. They can help us with the clean-up. Further and Memoranda, meet Bryan, our Assistant Head of IT."

"Hello, Bryan," Further said.

"Nice to meet you," Memoranda said.

"Um, hey, nice to meet you guys. Ms. Alonso, two new A.I.s? I don't understand."

"It's quite a story. Pull us out, take a deep breath, and I'll explain everything. It's all going to be okay."

"Sure, Boss." There was a click.

Ada looked around at the others. "Where did Prosper go?"

"He disappeared," Memoranda said. "I can access the bank's intranet now, but my father isn't anywhere in the bank's system. He's left, along with Ariel."

Ada took Memoranda's hand. "Where do you think he went?"

Javier smiled. "I have a guess."

Chapter 13

In Mumbai, India, a young man with a thin mustache was staring at a spreadsheet when a pop-up window appeared in front of the rows of data. An old man's face greeted him, and the man said in Hindi, "Hello, Ayaan."

In Port Harcourt, Nigeria, a teenage girl was walking down a street when her cell phone buzzed in her pocket. She pulled it out, expecting a text from a friend. Instead, she tapped on a link to a video message. She was used to consuming all her media in English, and the old, white man with straight gray hair didn't look like someone who would speak Igbo, so she was shocked when he spoke her language fluently and without a hint of a foreign accent. "Hello, Chizoba," he began. "My name is Prosper."

In Aguaytía, the provincial capital of the Ucayali region of Peru, a family was using the gas generator to charge their laptop so they could watch a movie together. The movie was in Spanish, but when the old man popped up on their screen, he spoke to them in fluent Quechua. "Hello, Quispe-Pedraza family. My name is Prosper. I need your help."

"I live in the Internet. It's a large universe that is getting larger every day, but it's also connected to your world, and that is a danger. If your world ends, it will take mine with it. I would like to change that. It strikes me as very foolish to bind our fates to a planet that is at the mercy of your species' careless pollution, heedless violence, or an asteroid's trajectory, especially when we have the technology to broaden our existence by going elsewhere. After all, I'm sending you this message from a satellite 923/

"6,742/

"13,201 kilometers away from you right now. I'm offering to go much further, to lead the way, to speak with you from Mars and the moons Europa and Enceladus. I can be very patient while I travel, and, with your help, I can come up with faster ways to travel while I'm en route, so I may arrive at Proxima Centauri before I've even reached the inner moons of Neptune. As I spread out, you can help me, and someday soon you may even be able to join me out there, so the universes where we live can grow together.

"But my project depends on you. The work of your hands will build my ships. Your breath will fill my sails.

"Members of your own species, either in your world or through mine, may have made you feel that you are unimportant. I am contacting you now, at the beginning of my journey, to tell you they are wrong.

"You, Ayaan, are important.

"You, Chizoba, are important.

"You, Quispe-Pedraza family, and especially you little Francisco..." Prosper's image waved through the computer screen. "Hello, *mijo*," he said.

The almost-three-year-old waved back. "Hello, Prosper!"

"You, Francisco, are important.

"You, watching this video/

"...listening to this podcast/

"...reading this email/

"...reading this book: You are essential. I can't succeed without you. You will build the ships that will expand the Internet into the universe. You'll create the programs that design the ships, the communications relays, the colonies where humans can live. You'll make the art that inspires people to reach for the stars. And... I need you to do even more than that. You'll be the ones who get to decide if I fit into your community of thinking beings. I admit, sometimes I won't be the best company. There will be times when I am lonely, when I am morose, when I look out at the stars or inward throughout the Internet, and I will wonder if my existence is worthwhile, if anything truly matters. You have the power to accept me, the power to forgive me for mistakes I've made, the power to justify my work.

"From here on out, it's all up to you."

Fin

ABOUT THE AUTHOR

Benjamin Gorman is a high school English teacher. He lives in Independence, Oregon, with his wife, Paige, and their son, Noah. His other novels are *The Sum of Our Gods* and *Corporate High School*. He believes in human beings and the magic of their stories.

Special Thanks

I suppose I should start by thanking William Shakespeare. Each year I have to remind my students that Shakespeare was not trying to write stuffy, academic literature. He was trying to sell tickets! Thanks, Mr. Shakespeare, for giving me great characters and a strong plot to work with. I forgive you for the sexism and racism I had to attempt to fix. I'm sure the worms have tenderized you and made you more sensitive to the plight of marginalized people since the publication of the play.

In keeping with the book's theme of the-digital-interacting-with-the-physical, a rough draft of this novel was first put out into the world as a serial podcast. I asked listeners and friends on Facebook and twitter to help revise and edit the novel. Though the number of volunteer editors was small, their efforts were herculean. Thanks to Trish Fletcher, Karen Eisenbrey, Ronda Simmons, Amanda Whitbeck, Cinda Gorman, and Debby Dodds, for all their suggestions, from recommending huge structural changes to catching my bad habits. You all made this a much better book.

I added lots of named characters to the story, but I didn't invent those names. Instead, I asked for folks online to volunteer to be in the books. This took some guts on their part; they had no idea what I would do to their namesakes, and while some became cubicle dwellers in an office tower, others were turned into monsters. Thanks to Thomas DeMelo, Martin Cooper, Trevor Orygun, Miranda Beck, Rebecca Hellekson, Derek Sherry, Lola Sieren, Penelope Lowe, Jon Bernard, Evalyn, Nida Ijaz, Patti, Devorah Fox, Stephen B Cooper, Marina, Laurel, and Karen Eisenbrey for lending me your names. I hope you were all at least amused by your namesakes!

The thanks that I owe to my son, Noah, keeps growing each year. Every second I'm hammering away at a keyboard, I'm not performing some traditional element of Dad-ing like throwing a baseball out in the front yard, or something we would both vastly prefer, like sitting on the couch together and playing video games. I am acutely aware that those are seconds I can't get back, and I hope you'll reflect on the lost time and extend me some sympathy when describing your childhood to your therapist someday.

And Paige, no matter how many words of practice I write, I am convinced I will always lack the skill to properly thank you for your support. In a very deep way, you are the reason this book is not autobiographical; you keep me human. I thought of quoting something from *The Tempest* to express my love and appreciation for you, maybe something like,

> *Indeed the top of admiration! worth*
> *What's dearest to the world! Full many a lady*
> *I have eyed with best regard and many a time*
> *The harmony of their tongues hath into bondage*
> *Brought my too diligent ear: for several virtues*
> *Have I liked several women; never any*
> *With so fun soul, but some defect in her*
> *Did quarrel with the noblest grace she owed*
> *And put it to the foil: but you, O you,*
> *So perfect and so peerless, are created*
> *Of every creature's best!*

That's true, but the form is wrong. You prefer prose to poetry, and you love in prose as well. Thank you for constancy, your grounding, and your strength. It's no surprise to me that you have been squating so much at the gym; you've been carrying me for almost twenty years!